FIRE ON THE MOUNTAIN

An imprint of Hendrickson Publishers Marketing, LLC.
Peabody, Massachusetts
www.HendricksonRose.com

FIRE ON THE MOUNTAIN

A
TIME CRASHERS
Adventure

BY

H. MICHAEL BREWER

DEDICATION:

For Janet: Thanks for the fire! (Song of Solomon 8:6-7)

TIME CRASHERS: FIRE ON THE MOUNTAIN

© 2014 by Michael Brewer

RoseKidz®
An imprint of Hendrickson Publishers Marketing, LLC.
P. O. Box 3473, Peabody
Massachusetts 01961-3473
www.HendricksonRose.com

Register your book at www. HendricksonRose.com/register and receive a free Bible Reference download.

Cover and interior illustrator: Aburtov and Graphikslava

ISBN 10: 1-58411-145-3
ISBN 13: 978-1-58411-145-0
RoseKidz® reorder #L48702
Juvenile Fiction / Religious / Christian / General

Printed in the United States of America   [05]   05.2017.VP

TABLE OF CONTENTS

FIRE ON THE MOUNTAIN

Introduction

ime travel… A crazy science-fiction dream? No! Thanks to the work of Dr. Benton Conway, now there is a path from the 21st century into history. Working in secrecy, the brilliant scientist has built a time machine in the laboratory hidden beneath the basement of his home. Dr. Conway has revealed his project only to his son Ethan. When the researcher suddenly goes missing, family housekeeper Miss Wigger assumes the scientist has been called away on business. Dr. Conway often travels for long periods, carrying out government missions.

But Ethan knows his father would never leave him without saying goodbye. Ethan is convinced Benton Conway has used the machine to send himself into the past—and has gotten into trouble. The scientist's son decides to locate his missing father and bring him safely back to the present. Using his father's notes,

TIME CRASHERS

Ethan learns to operate the time machine. The device is pre-programmed for 33 trips into the mysterious past, and each trip really is a mystery. Ethan has no idea where the programming will send him, but he is certain that if he keeps trying, one of the time journeys will lead to his father.

Fortunately, Ethan doesn't travel alone. Jake Bradley, a natural athlete, and Spencer Price, a young genius, are friends closer than brothers. They will accompany Ethan into the past no matter where it leads.

And you will take part in the adventure, too. You'll jump into history with Ethan, Jake, and Spencer. You'll face the same dangers, and you'll help them make life-or-death decisions. How this story turns out is up to you! Maybe you'll come face to face with samurai warriors or sabre tooth tigers or Attila the Hun. Only this much is certain: how the story unfolds is up to you. Your decisions will shape the adventure and decide the ending.

If you don't like adventure and risk, if you're afraid to take chances, close this book right now! But if you're willing to lay it all on the line to help Ethan find his dad, read on. If you're ready to look danger in the eye, you've come to the right place. If you want to help the Time Crashers make it safely home, take a deep breath . . . and turn the page.

$\Longrightarrow$ **DON'T SAY YOU WEREN'T WARNED!**

Warm Cookies

"**T**ake this plate of chocolate chip cookies," Miss Wigger says with a cheery smile. "You can't do homework on an empty stomach."

"Thanks," Ethan Conway says, accepting the sweet-smelling goodies.

Miss Wigger became the live-in housekeeper years ago when Ethan's mother died. Ethan barely remembers his real mother, and the housekeeper is like his second mom. She doesn't know that Ethan's dad has disappeared, lost in the past. Dr. Conway travels on secret projects for the government, often for weeks at a time. Miss Wigger thinks he is away on a business trip—so far. Ethan has to find his father before anyone gets suspicious. If the authorities discover Dr. Conway is missing, they will put Ethan in a foster home. The time machine hidden in the sub-basement of their house will be out of reach. Without the machine, Ethan has no hope of rescuing his father.

"What kind of project is this?" Miss Wigger asks.

"History," says Spencer Price, one of Ethan's closest friends. Spencer is like a computer chip, small but crammed with information.

"Nobody in history makes cookies like yours, Miss Wigger," Jake Bradley adds, snatching a warm one from the plate. Jake is Ethan's other best friend, an all-around athlete and the tallest of the trio. Jake yearns for action and adventure.

The housekeeper laughs and waves the boys down the basement steps. "Save the sweet-talking for your teacher. Maybe you'll get an A on that history project."

In the basement, Ethan hands the cookies to Spencer and opens a closet. He presses his open hand to a glass plate in the wall. A mechanical voice drones, "Conway, Ethan. Palm print identification confirmed. Please proceed." The closet's rear wall slides away, revealing another flight of stairs leading to a room dimly illuminated by red light.

As the boys enter Dr. Conway's hidden lab, the door seals

behind them. The time machine is a huge device, a horseshoe shaped machine that fills three walls of the underground room. A glowing crystal, the power source for the time machine, bathes the boys in ruby light.

"I'll never get used to this," Spencer says in a hushed voice. "Your dad is such a genius."

"A missing genius," Ethan says. "I studied Dad's notes, and I've learned more about the machine. On our last trip, we could only spend thirty hours in the past."

"Sure," Jake mumbles around a mouthful of cookie. "At the place we appear in the past, once each hour the time machine sends a removal bus to bring us home."

Spencer rolls his eyes. "Not removal bus," he says through gritted teeth. "Retrieval pulse!"

"Yeah, that's what I said," Jake continues. "The removal bus will bring us home, but after thirty hours the machine shuts down and we're left in the past."

"If we miss the last RETRIEVAL PULSE," Spencer adds, nearly shouting the words at Jake, "we're history."

"Except I've figured out how to keep the pulses coming for two days," Ethan explains. "We'll have forty-eight hours before we're stranded in the past."

"Excellent!" Jake says. "If only we had that extra eighteen hours

on the last trip."

"Yeah," Spencer agrees. "An extra eighteen hours to swim in freezing water or run from Vikings or fight wild boars."

"Eighteen more hours crawling in a mud pit or staring down hungry wolves," Jake says, rubbing his hands enthusiastically. "Boy, we got cheated on that last time trip. I want my money back!"

"Why are my friends such losers?" Ethan moans, flinging his hands toward the low ceiling. "If you guys had been with Columbus, he would have turned around and sailed home just to get rid of you."

"We're punking you," Jake says, wrapping his pal in a bear hug. "It was a great trip. I raced a Viking and got stabbed by a spear. How amazing is that?"

"And we saved one of the world's most precious books," Spencer adds with pride.

"It's always about books with you," Jake says to Spencer, shaking his head. "On the Cool-O-Meter, I'm a hundred and you're maybe three-and-a-half. But stick with me and my awesomeness might rub off on you."

Spencer waves a hand at Jake's outfit: cargo pants and a photographer's vest, the pockets stuffed with emergency supplies. "Did you say Cool-O-Meter or Fool-O-Meter?"

Jake snatches the last cookie, swallows contentedly, and says,

"You just fell from three-and-a-half to two-and-a-half for making fun of my superhero-style utility vest. I wonder if the Cool-O-Meter registers negative numbers?"

 TURN TO **PAGE 14**.

DIFFERENT STROKES

Jake and Spencer like to kid about their differences. They know that our differences are part of God's plan. God gives us different gifts and talents so we can work together and help each other. To read the verse, scratch out every J, Q, Z and X from the letters below.

T J H Q E X Z R E A J R E Z X D I F Q F J E Z R E N Q T K Z I J N Q D
X S O Z F G I F Q T J S Z , B J U Q X T Z T H E S Q Z A M J E S Z P J
I R Q I X T Z D I J S T Z R J I B Q U T E X Z S J T Z H Q E M .
J T Z H E X R Q E A R Z E J D Q I X F Z F E J R Q E N X J Z T K I
Q N D Z S X O Q F S E Z R V Q I C J Z E , B J U Z Q T X T Z H Q E S
A Z M X E Q L O Z R J D .   (1 Corinthians 12:4-5)

Write the sentences here:

_____

_____

_____

_____

                                        (1 Corinthians 12:4-5)

SEE ANSWERS ON PAGE 199.

Cookie break is officially over," Ethan announces, trying not to grin at his pals' endless squabbling. "Let's roll."

They position themselves on a metal plate in the concrete floor, the time machine wrapped around them. Ethan presses a green button on the control panel. The button blinks, lazily at first, then rapidly.

"Get ready!" Ethan shouts over the humming of the machine.

Ethan's shoulders hunch as a familiar vibration tingles his spine. His skin prickles as if mice are tap-dancing on his arms and face. The power crystal blazes, painting the lab the color of blood. Ethan swallows uncomfortably, thankful he didn't eat as many cookies as Jake. The shrill hum pounds his aching ears, louder than a jet engine. Just when he fears that his eyeballs might pop from his head, the noise dies.

The basement lab vanishes. Slanting rays of warm sunshine replace the ruddy light. Under their feet, instead of cold cement,

thick grass rises ankle high. Gnarled trees with twisted trunks surround them. The gentle "baa" of a sheep floats through the still air.

"Where are we?" Jake asks.

"And when are we?" Spencer echoes.

Behind them, not more than four or five miles away, a mountain blots out the sky. Groves of trees and gardens decorate the gentle slopes. Closer at hand, a city nestles on a plain falling toward the sea. The sun hangs above the blue ocean.

"Is it morning or afternoon?" Spencer wonders.

Jake fumbles in a vest pocket and draws out a compass. He points toward the ocean and says, "That's west, so it must be later in the day." He grins triumphantly at Spencer and pockets the compass.

"Wow! This place is beautiful," Ethan says.

"So is a coral snake," Spencer replies. "I can't put my finger on it, but danger is in the air."

Ethan nods thoughtfully. "On our last trip we arrived in the middle of a battle. Nobody had much reason to notice us," he says. "Let's try not to draw attention. Asking what city we're in and what year it is will make us stick out like a chocolate bar in the mashed potatoes."

"We go in like ninja spies," Jake agrees, striking a karate pose. "We move like shadows."

"Yeah, you'll blend right in," Spencer mumbles, glancing sideways at the athlete's jacket and vest. "Maybe you can use the invisibility cloak in pocket number 29."

"You're still depressed," Jake says, squeezing the smaller boy's shoulder, "because the library won't let you borrow more than twenty books at a time."

"If Dad came here, I'm sure he went that way," Ethan says, pointing toward the city. "Let's get our bearings. We have to be on this spot to catch the retrieval pulse that will take us home."

"These olive trees are planted in even rows," Spencer observes. "If we let that tree on the corner represent the zero point on a geometry axis, then this tree we're under is…" He pauses to count. "This would be tree 5, 19."

"And how are we supposed to remember that?" Jake asks skeptically.

"Easy," Spencer answers. "Standing under this tree will get us back to the 21st century right? So we just remember Mark 5:19 where Jesus says, 'Go home to your own people.'"

"You can have your math mumbo jumbo," Jake says smugly. He tugs a small can of spray paint from a bulging pocket and marks an

TIME CRASHERS

orange X on the ground.

"I hope sheep don't like orange grass," Ethan quips.

As the boys walk toward the town, Ethan passes a picture of his father to each friend. Originally a photo, Ethan used his computer to turn it into a sketch.

"Show these around to see if anyone remembers Dad," Ethan explains.

"Good idea," Jake says. "A drawing won't make people suspicious, but a digital photo would stand out like a… What did you say? Like licorice in rice pudding?"

"Close enough," Ethan chuckles. "Spence, can you scope anything?"

His eyes very focused, Spencer says, "I'd guess we're somewhere around the Mediterranean Sea. That's a Roman city, large enough for 20,000 or 30,000 people. The common language is either Latin or Greek, but we don't have to worry about that. The language app on the time machine teaches us the local language wherever we go. The gates are open; that means peaceful times. But guards are on duty, so we can count on Roman law and order. There's a lot of activity in the city. Maybe it's a festival or holiday."

"Anything else?" Ethan asks.

"Christians might not be popular," Spencer says. "Christianity eventually converted the Roman Empire, but at first Christians were hated. Roman swords spilled a lot of Christian blood."

"I'm not going to lie about being a Christian," Jake says fiercely.

"Just don't broadcast it," Spencer warns. "There's no need to sing 'Jesus Loves Me' as we pass the guards."

The three fall silent as they pass through the city gate. A soldier eyes them curiously. The guard wears a rounded helmet with cheek guards. Armor made of metal plates covers his chest and shoulders, over a short-sleeved tunic that falls to the middle of his thigh. His feet planted in thick-soled sandals, short sword hanging from his belt, and spear gripped in his right hand, the soldier looks like a fighting machine.

"No wonder Rome conquered most of the world," Jake whispers.

DRESS FOR SUCCESS!

The armor and weapons of Roman soldiers helped them conquer the ancient world. Did you know that Christians have armor, too? God gives us spiritual armor to help us overcome problems and temptations. Read what the Bible says about this armor and then fill in the blanks pointing to the soldier's armor on page 22. Draw your own face in the Christian armor!

"Therefore put on the full armor of God, so that when the day of evil comes, you may be able to stand your ground, and after you have done everything, to stand. Stand firm then, with the belt of truth buckled around your waist, with the breastplate of righteousness in place, and with your feet fitted with the readiness that comes from the gospel of peace. In addition to all this, take up the shield of faith, with which you can extinguish all the flaming arrows of the evil one.

TIME CRASHERS

Take the helmet of salvation and the sword of the Spirit, which is the word of God. And pray in the Spirit on all occasions with all kinds of prayers and requests." (Ephesians 6:13-18)

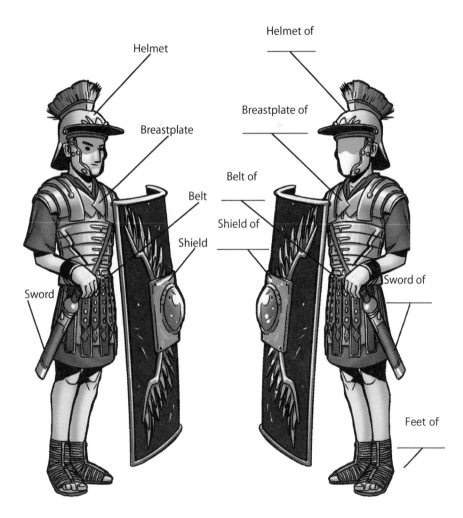

Helmet

Breastplate

Belt

Shield

Sword

Helmet of
_____

Breastplate of
_____

Belt of
_____

Shield of
_____

Sword of

Feet of
_____

SEE ANSWERS ON PAGE 199.

s the guard measures the boys, he slowly nods.

"From the look of your clothes, you've come from far away," he guesses. He nods at Spencer. "We don't see many Africans here. Are you free men or slaves?"

"Free men," Ethan answers.

"Lucanus Honorius of the city guard bids you welcome," the guard growls thumping one fist over his heart. "Enjoy the Feast of Vulcan. And stay out of trouble."

"Feast of Vulcan, a city by the sea, a big mountain…" Spencer mumbles. "Alarm bells are ringing, but I can't figure it out." He shakes his head as if to rattle his brain. "Something bad is in the air, guys."

"It'll come to you, Spence," Ethan says. The sky is blue, the sun is shining, the people of the city appear happy and friendly. What could go wrong?

The wide streets bustle with men in togas, robed women whose arms are heavy with gold bracelets, and youngsters in short tunics. The city rings with the cry of food sellers, barking dogs, neighing horses, and clattering carts.

"Ah, the Roman aroma," Spencer declares, breathing deeply. "I smell charcoal smoke, fresh bread, cooking meat, and wine." He turns his face slowly, sniffing. "Fish. Horse sweat. Leather. And…" His nose wrinkles. "And something that should have been flushed." He steps back from the murky water trickling through the streets.

"Do you think there's a stadium with athletic games?" Jake wondered.

"Or a library?" Spencer asks.

As they walk along, the street opens into a broad, paved square large enough for several football fields.

"The Forum," Spencer says. "The heart of any Roman city."

Pillared buildings of white marble surround the Forum. Spencer studies the statues and carvings on the buildings. "That looks like a temple for Jupiter, the king of the Roman gods. And over there a temple for Apollo, the sun god."

"How many gods do the Romans worship?" Ethan asks.

"The Romans have more gods than Jake has pockets," Spencer grins.

A man wearing an iron ankle bracelet squeezes between the boys, bent beneath a bale of wool.

"The finest wool in the Empire," he shouts. "Here in the trading house of Eumachia." He beckons with his head before disappearing through a stone arch.

"Let's get busy," Ethan says.

"What the strategy, boss?" Jake asks.

"Don't call me boss," Ethan says. He doesn't like taking charge. If something goes wrong, it will be his fault. Finding his father, keeping his friends safe, getting them home again, all of it weighs on his shoulders like a backpack full of bricks.

"What's the plan, leader man?" Jake asks.

"Don't call me leader man," Ethan insists, sounding annoyed.

"Come on, call the play, Ethan," Jake continues, grinning now.

"Don't call me Eth—" Ethan breaks off while his pals laugh. He takes a deep breath and relaxes.

"Okay, you got me," Ethan admits. "There's a lot of ground to cover. We'll split up."

"Does that mean I won't have to paw through a bunch of dusty scrolls with the book-worm?" Jake asks.

"And I won't be bored to death watching chariot races with Jake the Jock?" Spencer adds.

"Keep moving," Ethan instructs. "Show Dad's picture. Ask

around for anyone dressed like us."

"Dressed like Jake?" Spencer says. "I don't think so."

"We'll meet here in the Forum," Ethan decides. "On the steps of Jupiter's temple."

Ethan extends one hand. The other two lay their hands on top of his.

"All for one," says Ethan.

"And one for all," Jake and Spencer answer.

"Look out, Rome!" Jake says. "The three time-traveling musketeers are on the job!"

IF YOU WANT TO FOLLOW ETHAN, SEE **PAGE 28**.

IF YOU WANT TO STICK WITH JAKE, TURN TO **PAGE 61**.

IF YOU WANT TO TAG ALONG WITH SPENCER, TURN TO **PAGE 80**.

s the shadows lengthen, Ethan basks in the warmth from sunbaked buildings. He approaches strangers with his father's picture, but no one remembers seeing a tall man with red hair and a birthmark on his cheek. Cupping water in his hand, Ethan drinks from a public fountain. He wipes his mouth and sets out to cross a busy avenue. The street is sunken below the level of the sidewalk and runs with stinky, black liquid, the drippings of garbage, rotted food, animal droppings, and sewage. Here and there, stepping-stones rise above the smelly slime for crossing with dry feet. As Ethan maps the best route across the avenue, he is pushed from behind.

"Make room for Vesonius Primus!" shouts a thickset man with sandy hair. He wears the short, rough tunic of a hired servant, strong arms and shoulders stretching the coarse fabric. Behind him is a stately man in a rich toga edged in purple. His skin is bronzed and a fringe of gray hair circles his smooth head. A young boy skips at his heels.

"Stand aside!" the servant snarls, seizing Ethan's arm and flinging him away.

As the servant glares at Ethan, the little boy dashes past them and leaps onto one of the stepping-stones in the street. He lands in front of a speeding horse-drawn wagon loaded with melons. The startled horse rears up. His front legs paw at the air. The little boy looks up in frozen fear as the heavy hooves fall toward him.

Brushing past the bullying servant, Ethan launches himself at the frightened child, grabbing the boy's tunic in one hand. The crushing hooves of the panicked horse crash down on the stepping-stone a split second after Ethan leaps backward, dragging the boy with him. The two tumble on the stone sidewalk. The boy wails in fear, while Ethan rubs his banged elbow.

The man in the fancy toga sweeps the screaming child into his arms, hugging him fiercely. The servant approaches, wringing his hands. With a bowed head, he says, "I'm so sorry, master."

Holding the boy in one arm, the older man slaps the cringing servant.

"Garius Chlorus," he roars, striking him again. "You worthless

dog! I told you to watch the boy!"

Garius Chlorus falls to his knees, cringing and covering his head. He points a trembling finger at Ethan. "He distracted me."

The angry man aims a kick at the servant, then extends his free hand to help Ethan rise.

"My nephew could have been killed," says the man in a cultured voice. "The friendship of Vesonius Primus is yours, young man. In this city that counts for a great deal."

"It was nothing, sir," Ethan says. "I'm glad I could help."

Still gripping his hand, Vesonius says, "Come home with me. We are having a banquet in honor of the festival of Vulcan. Please be my guest."

Vesonius Primus seems wealthy, and his banquet will probably include other important people, the kind of people who might know about his father. But Ethan remembers that these Roman feasts can last for hours. He might better spend the time searching. Also, he is uncomfortable with the hateful stare of Garius Chlorus.

 IF YOU THINK ETHAN SHOULD GO TO THE BANQUET, SEE **PAGE 32.**

IF YOU THINK ETHAN SHOULD TURN DOWN THE INVITATION, GO TO **PAGE 51.**

Making up his mind, Ethan squeezes the rich man's hand. "I'd love to have dinner in your home."

"Wonderful!" Vesonius says heartily. Glaring at Garius Chlorus kneeling on the stone pavement, the older man growls, "Get up! Finish your errands and meet us back at the fullery."

"Yes, Lord," Chlorus whimpers. He scurries away, head ducked. He aims another angry stare at Ethan.

"What is a fullery?" Ethan asks as Vesonius guides him, still carrying the red-eyed child.

"Wool is an important business around here," the man explains. "A fullery is a place to wash and prepare wool cloth to become clothing and blankets. It must be treated, shrunken, and stretched before going to market. My fullery has made me wealthy."

Vesonius fixes Ethan in his gaze. "And what brings you to our fair city, young sir?"

Ethan offers the picture of his father. "I'm looking for this man."

The fuller studies the picture.

"Do I see a family resemblance?" he asks.

"He's my father," Ethan admits.

Vesonius nods, eyes fixed on the picture. "Would he be dressed in the same manner as you and your two friends?"

Shocked, Ethan blurts, "How do you know about my friends?"

Vesonius laughs. "At the public baths, first we clean our ears, then we fill them with gossip." His smile vanishes. "I've heard nothing of your father, but I will ask my friends at dinner."

Arriving at a large building with a red-tiled roof, Vesonius announces, "Welcome to my home."

Ethan points to carefully painted letters on the wall near the arched doorway: VESONIUS PRIMUS URGES THE ELECTION OF GNAEUS HELVIUS, A MAN WORTHY OF PUBLIC OFFICE.

"Yes, we use the walls of the city to express our ideas," the fuller says. "Is that not the practice in your land?"

Ethan thinks of graffiti sprayed on bridges, overpasses, train cars, and billboards. "Uh, I guess so. What's this?" He points to scattered letters scrawled on the pavement.

"Those are numbers used in some children's game," Vesonius explains.

TAKE A NUMBER!

The Romans used letters for numbers. Take a look at the chart below, and you'll see which letters stood for which numbers.

I = 1   V = 5   X = 10   L = 50   C = 100   D = 500   M = 1,000

Let's see if you can figure out these jokes and riddles using Roman numerals. Warning! Some of these are very corny. Hint: For these riddles, use the letters, not the Roman numbers.

Which Roman numeral can climb a wall?

Which Roman numeral belongs on top of a jar?

Which Roman numeral plays music?

Which Roman numeral needs a new light bulb?

Which Roman numeral did the blind man shout when Jesus healed him?

What is the favorite Roman numeral of the retired doctor?

Which Roman numeral did the police officer ask for?

Which Roman numeral is a word in a recipe?

BRAIN TEASER: Can you translate this Roman numeral into a regular number? (If you have trouble, you can find the number in your Bible at Genesis 5:27.):

CMLXIX

Hint: When a smaller number comes right before a bigger number, subtract the smaller from the larger. So V is five and I is one, but IV is four.   **SEE ANSWERS ON PAGES 199-200.**

than's host ushers him into a room decorated by drawings of people and animals. When Ethan looks closer he sees that the art is made of tiny, colored tiles cemented to the walls and floor.

"Excuse me while I change clothes," Vesonius Primus says to Ethan. A middle-aged woman approaches and kisses Vesonius on the cheek. She is thin and elegant. A gold bracelet encircles her wrist, a yellow serpent swallowing its tail. "My wife Cornelia will make you welcome."

"You must be the young hero who plucked our nephew out of danger," she greets Ethan.

"News travels fast," Ethan says.

Cornelia laughs. She notices Ethan studying a niche in the wall, a recessed area no larger than a pizza box. A scene is painted there. Two figures hold drinking cups and a third figure is poised between them. A fat snake wriggles beneath their feet.

"Our family shrine," Cornelia explains. "I wanted the goddess Isis, but Vesonius put his foot down. Which god do you prefer, Ethan?"

Ethan remembers Spencer's warning that Christianity might not be legal in this city. "Uh, I worship the Son," he tells her.

"Ah, yes," Cornelia agrees. "The sun god Apollo. Always a good choice."

Ethan remains silent. He has told the truth; if she misunderstands, that isn't his fault.

As they stroll through a marble hallway, Ethan spots Garius Chlorus carrying a heavy basket of pomegranates and cucumbers. Cornelia claps her hands and the sulky servant kneels.

"Leave those," the hostess says. "Take care of our guest, while I make sure everything is ready for the feast."

Garius Chlorus lowers the basket of vegetables with a grunt. "Please follow me, sir," he says in a friendly tone, but his eyes are resentful.

They pass through an outdoor courtyard where people mingle

and servants are spreading tables with food. Ethan is surprised when Chlorus brings him to the stables behind the house where a chariot gleams with polish. The carriage is made of strips of woven wood and leather, painted red and purple. Two gray stallions are harnessed to the chariot, tall, muscled, and eager.

"My master wishes to honor you," Garius Chlorus sneers. "You are to drive his parade chariot. When you arrive in front of the house, Vesonius Primus will bring out his guests to salute you."

Ethan's heart flips and flops as he circles the chariot. This is cooler than a Corvette, cooler than a Jaguar, cooler than…anything! He doesn't know how to drive a chariot, but how hard could it be?

 IF YOU THINK ETHAN SHOULD DRIVE THE CHARIOT, CONTINUE TO **PAGE 39**.

 IF YOU THINK ETHAN SHOULD SAY NO TO THE CHARIOT RIDE, TURN TO **PAGE 46**.

The horses know what to do, Ethan reassures himself. If it were dangerous, Vesonius Primus wouldn't invite him. He steps gingerly into the chariot, settling his feet carefully and taking the reins. Garius Chlorus grips the harness, saying, "I'll lead you into the street."

The horses' hooves clop on paving stones and the chariot clatters behind them, slow but bouncy. Ethan pictures himself rolling up in the chariot while Vesonius Primus and his guests applaud. The surly servant leads the chariot through narrow alleys into a broad avenue. People gape at Ethan standing proudly in the chariot, head held high and reins draped loosely in one hand.

"I hope you enjoy the ride, young sir." Garius Chlorus practically spits the last words. He lifts a heavy hand and slaps the nearer horse

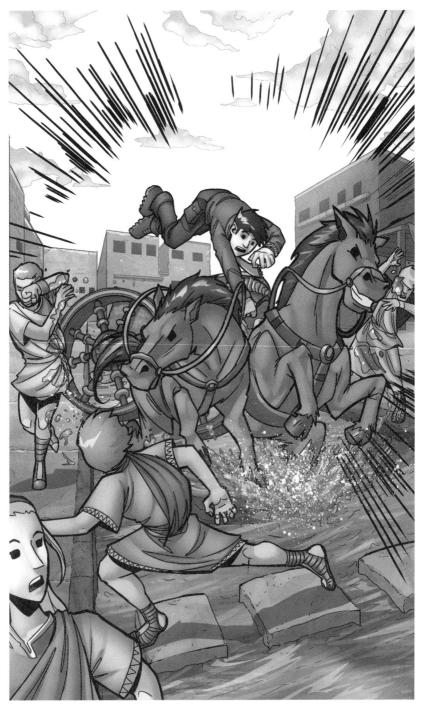

on the rump. Both horses rear, threatening to throw Ethan from the chariot, then they bolt away like lightning. The chariot jounces and bounces wildly. Ethan loses the reins, which fall over the front of the cart and drag behind the horses. Clutching desperately, Ethan fights to remain in the careening chariot. Behind him, Garius Chlorus shouts, "Thief! Thief! He's stealing the master's chariot! Someone stop him!"

The stallions gallop madly. Foamy patches of sweat dampen their gray hides. Stinking wastewater splashes on Ethan's legs as he squints against the wind. In the street ahead, people leap aside, screaming and jostling to escape.

Ethan shouts "Whoa!" but the cry spooks the horses into wilder flight. He leans over the front of the chariot, straining to reach the whipping reins. As his fingertips brush the leather cords, an unexpected bounce flips him halfway from the carriage, his face dangling inches from the pounding rear hooves.

WILD WHEELS

One of the kings of Israel was known for his crazy chariot driving. Who is the wildest driver in the Bible? When a guard saw this man driving a chariot toward the city gate, here is what he said:

_____ _____ _____ _____ _____ _____ _____

_____ _____ _____; _____ _____ _____ _____ _____.

To fill in the blanks, read the word wheel. Start with the circled letter and move to the right (clockwise) reading every second letter. (So the first word will be THE.) By the time you've gone around the wheel twice, you'll have the whole message from 2 Kings 9:20.

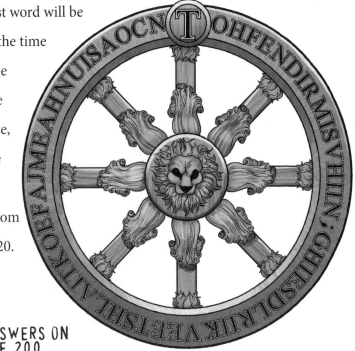

SEE ANSWERS ON PAGE 200.

Ethan struggles back into the chariot as the horses hurtle into a broad intersection. Directly in their path, a donkey wagon loaded with firewood rattles across the street. The driver leaps from the wagon, but the donkey maintains his plodding pace. At the last instant, the gray stallions veer right. The chariot tips over, balancing on one wheel for twenty yards, then falls in a crash that splinters woven wood slats and bursts leather straps. The harnesses broken, the horses gallop away while the wreckage of the chariot slides to a stop. Ethan scrambles from the remains of the chariot, unharmed except for a few bruises and bumps.

An angry crowd gathers. Thinking fast, Ethan shouts, "He nearly ran me down! Call the guard! I think he went down that alley."

A gang of men run in the direction Ethan points, and others mill around in curiosity. Ethan limps away as quickly as he can move without raising suspicion. Maybe he should return to the home of

Vesonius Primus to explain what happened. But who knows if the old Roman will believe Ethan or the lying Garius Chlorus? He slams a fist into his palm. He'd like to meet Garius Chlorus again. He has a few things to settle with the servant who framed him for stealing a chariot and nearly got him killed.

A moment later, he gets his wish when he turns a corner and confronts the treacherous servant. The man is panting and red-faced. He must have been chasing the runaway chariot through the streets. Ethan is so angry as he reaches for Garius Chlorus that he fails to see the Roman guard at the servant's side.

"There he is!" Chlorus shouts, leaping backward before Ethan can grab the front of his tunic.

A steely hand drops on Ethan's shoulder. He looks up into the piercing eyes of Lucanus Honorius.

"You're the guard from the city gate," Ethan sputters.

"I told you to stay out of trouble, foreigner. You should have listened."

"I didn't do anything wrong!" Ethan protests.

"It's your word against the word of Vesonius Primus, one of our foremost citizens," Lucanus grunts. "Who do think I'm going to believe?"

"Garius Chlorus is lying about me," Ethan insists.

The guard glances at Garius Chlorus who smiles smugly.

"Perhaps. I know this Chlorus. He is more slippery than an oiled eel. We'll sort it out tomorrow," Lucanus promises, "but tonight you sleep in the city jail."

Lucanus Honorius orders Garius Chlorus to catch up with the runaway horses and return them to his master's stable. Then he marches Ethan through busy streets as bystanders point and mutter. In a few minutes, they reach a courtyard where sweating athletes run laps. Others hurl spears at targets or spar with blunt wooden swords.

"The training school for gladiators," the Roman guard explains. He nods toward a long stone building. "That is the barracks for the gladiators and also the jail."

TURN TO **PAGE 59**.

Ethan feels uneasy about the chariot ride, unsure if he can trust Garius Chlorus.

"I don't think I'm ready to drive a chariot," Ethan says, looking at the gray stallions with regret.

"This is an insult to Vesonius Primus," Chlorus snaps. "You have to do this or he will be angry."

"I'll explain it to him," Ethan offers.

"No, no," the servant says, suddenly worried. "No need to mention it to him. I'll smooth it over for you."

As Chlorus leads Ethan back to the feast, the servant glances at Ethan's jacket. "Your garment is soiled," he says, pulling a damp rag from his tunic. "Let me clean you up before you join the banquet." He seizes Ethan's jacket in thick, blunt fingers, dabbing at different spots. Ethan wonders if he has misjudged the man.

In the courtyard, several round tables are surrounded by short sofas where guests recline on one elbow, the other hand free to reach for food. Ethan settles on a soft cushion beside a pudgy man who stares at Ethan's clothes and rolls his eyes.

A slave kneels near Ethan and offers to fill his plate. She points to trays spread across the crowded table. "Pickled mushrooms," she says, "nettles cooked in vinegar, stewed snails." She looks at him expectantly, but he shakes his head.

"Baked dormice, grilled thrush birds, or delicious peacock tongues?" she offers. "No? Maybe a swan wing or a baby rabbit."

The slave brightens as four servants carry a huge tray into the middle of the room. The girl claps in delight. "The Trojan pig!" she exclaims.

On the tray is a whole roasted pig, standing on its feet. With a swing of his knife, one of the servants slices the animal's belly and an avalanche of sausages and fruits tumbles out. Ethan's stomach clinches and he swallows hard. To the slave girl he says, "Can I have a cup of water and a piece of bread?"

The girl bows and hurries away. As he waits for her to return, Ethan notices Garius Chlorus whispering in the ear of Vesonius Primus. Both look in his direction, and the older Roman scowls. Vesonius climbs to his feet and moves through the crowd, chatting

and nodding, until he reaches Ethan. With a forced smile, the older man offers a hand and raises Ethan from the couch.

"Please come with me," he says softly. With one arm around Ethan's shoulder, the Roman nobleman steers him to a small room. Suddenly, Vesonius shoves his hand into the pocket of Ethan's jacket. He pulls out a gold necklace with a ruby pendant.

"So Garius Chlorus spoke the truth," he says, eyes flashing. "You come into my home, accept my hospitality, and steal from me."

"I don't know how that necklace got into my pocket," Ethan protests. As the words leave his lips, he realizes the truth. Chlorus must have planted the jewelry in his pocket when he cleaned Ethan's jacket.

"Get out!" Vesonius Primus barks. "My servant has gone to fetch the city guard. Perhaps you can get out of the gates before they catch you. I owe you that much for saving my nephew, but nothing more."

Without another word, Ethan runs from the house. When he pauses to figure out which direction is best, Garius Chlorus leaps on his back and smashes him to the pavement.

"Get me in trouble with my master," he snarls. "Here's what you get in return." His big fists pound on Ethan. The boy kicks his way free, tries to run, but the servant grabs his foot and drags him down again. As they roll on the stones, a commanding voice rings out.

"Enough! Get to your feet!"

A Roman soldier stands over them, sword drawn. Ethan

recognizes him as Lucanus Honorius, the guard he met at the city gate. By now, Vesonius Primus has emerged from the house.

"This man stole from me," the nobleman declares, pointing a solemn finger at Ethan.

The Roman soldier raises a questioning eyebrow.

"It's a mistake," Ethan says.

"Of course he denies it," Chlorus says. "He knows the penalty for thievery is public execution."

"I must return to my guests," Vesonius explains. "I will come to the jail tomorrow to bring charges."

"Come along, foreigner." Lucanus Honorius grips Ethan's arm. "You should have taken my advice to stay out of trouble."

The Roman soldier leads him through a maze of streets. Drunken singing floats through the afternoon air. After walking several blocks, Lucanus Honorius and his prisoner pass a dusty lot where perspiring athletes practice swordplay. The Roman soldier stops at a nearby building.

TURN TO **PAGE 59**.

Thank you, Mr. Vesonius, but I'm not here for fun." Ethan shows his father's picture to the balding noble. "I'm looking for this man."

Vesonius studies the picture, lips pursed. Handing it back, he shakes his head. "Would this man be dressed in clothes like yours?" When Ethan nods, he continues, "If a man came into the city dressed so oddly, there would be rumors, but I have heard nothing."

Seeing Ethan's disappointment, Vesonius Primus returns the picture with a gold coin. "Accept a small gift for your courage," he says. "Please use my name if it will help in your search."

The elderly Roman turns toward his servant and boxes his ear. The man falls to one knee, rubbing the side of his head. "As for you, Garius Chlorus," Vesonius snaps, "you may thank the gods my nephew wasn't killed. If he had been, you would have followed him to the underworld. Go to the Forum and finish your errands before I decide to have you whipped like a dog!"

Ethan feels sorry for Garius Chlorus scampering away, head ducked like a beaten animal. Ethan heads in the same direction as the servant, deciding the Forum—the public square—is a good place to look for his father.

Festive crowds amble through the Forum, people of all ages buying and selling. A white-haired man recites poetry to cheering listeners, while nearby an armored warrior shouts an invitation to the gladiator games. Mingled with the smells of animals, perfume, and smoke, Ethan sniffs the scent of food. He spots a crowded cafeteria. A long counter contains sunken clay pots filled with different foods. Some of the foods are hot, others are chilled. Ethan wonders how the Romans can do this without heaters or refrigerators. These people are smarter than he thought.

Behind the counter, a serving woman with crooked teeth welcomes Ethan. "You have come to the right place, young sir, for the city's finest food."

Ethan holds up the coin. "Is this enough to buy a meal?"

"I see you're a stranger," the woman says, gray eyes gleaming. "For you, I offer the traveler's price, so yes, this will be enough." She plucks the coin and tucks it out of sight. Dipping a ladle into a steaming pot, she fills a bowl.

"Puls," she says, "porridge made from grain, fat, and water. And just for you," she offers a mischievous wink, "an extra treat of wild boar sausages." She plops the brown sausages into the thick goop. "What kind of wine?" she asks.

"Can I have a cup of milk?" Ethan asks.

The woman's eyebrows rise. "To drink?" she asks in amazement, and several diners turn to stare at Ethan.

"Just joking," Ethan says uncomfortably. "Is water okay?"

She fills a clay cup and slides it across the counter along with a bronze spoon. "Don't forget the spices," she adds, pointing to a collection of bowls containing salt and ground herbs. Ethan inspects a bowl of thick, strong-smelling sauce uncertainly.

"That's garum," the waitress explains helpfully, "made by Umbricius Scaurus. It's the best in the world."

"But what is it?" Ethan asks.

"Sauce made from the crushed guts of eels and mackerel fish, salted and aged in the sun for months, then squeezed and—"

"Darn," Ethan says, "it smells, uh, so good, but I'm allergic to fish guts."

The waitress shakes her head, dismay in her eyes as Ethan sits on a bench near the door. The goopy cereal reminds him of salty paste, but the wild pig sausages are juicy and tasty. He finishes them and gulps the water, listening to snatches of conversation.

A rough voice says, "Fish are dying in the Sarno River, floating on the water like leaves. It's a bad sign."

"My cousin herds sheep near the mountain," another man adds. "He says smelly steam leaks from the ground."

"The gods are angry," a third voice suggests. "Another earthquake is coming."

"We haven't finished rebuilding since the last quake seventeen years ago."

"Maybe an earthquake," says the gruff first voice. "Maybe something worse."

"What's worse than an earthquake?" snorts a skeptical speaker.

"Wait and see," replies the first man.

The conversation worries Ethan. He decides to get busy looking for his father. Returning his dishes to the counter, he shows the serving woman his father's picture. She sucks on her uneven teeth in deep thought, but she doesn't recognize Dr. Conway.

"Come back tomorrow," she urges Ethan. "Nowhere else will you find excellent food for such a price. Ask for Aeliana."

As Ethan turns toward the door, he glimpses the servant

Garius Chlorus skulking outside the café. When Ethan looks in his direction, Chlorus ducks behind a pillar. Is the servant following him? Uneasily, Ethan leaves the restaurant, pausing briefly at the spice bowls, then pushing into the crowded street.

Scarcely has he joined the flow of people before a hand clamps on his upper arm with a bruising grip. "Give me that gold coin," Garius Chlorus demands. "I have a knife, and I will use it."

"I don't have the coin," Ethan informs him, wincing at the bruising grip. "I spent it for lunch."

Chlorus's eyes bulge in horror. "You spent a gold aureus for a bowl of porridge? No one could be that stupid."

No wonder the waitress was so friendly. Garius Chlorus wants to rob Ethan with a knife, but Aeliana the waitress has already robbed him with a spoon.

"Are you stupid enough to stab me in front of a crowd?" Ethan challenges Garius Chlorus.

"No one will even see the blade," Chlorus threatens. He closes on Ethan, one hand inside his tunic.

Twisting in the servant's grip, Ethan spins and opens the hand that he dipped into a spice bowl as he left the café. A cloud of black pepper flies into Chlorus's face. The enraged man screeches as the blinding pepper stings his eyes. He inhales the pepper and sneezes violently. Between sneezes he shouts, "Thief! This foreigner is trying to rob me!"

As he rubs his running eyes, a thin dagger falls to the pavement, but Garius Chlorus keeps his other hand clinched on Ethan's arm.

"Guard!" Chlorus bellows. "Help!"

The crowd draws away from Ethan and Garius Chlorus. A Roman soldier bursts through the circle. Dashing tears from his red eyes, Chlorus shouts, "This foreigner tried to rob me!" He points to the dagger on the street and adds, "He threatened me with that knife."

"Come with me," the soldier orders Ethan. At the sound of his voice, Ethan recognizes the guard from the city gate.

"Lucanus Honorius," Ethan argues. "He's lying."

"My master the honorable Vesonius Primus will vouch for me," Garius Chlorus sneers. "Who will vouch for you?"

"I am a friend to Vesonius," Ethan insists.

Lucanus Honorius eyes him skeptically. "You arrived in the city this afternoon, and you've already befriended one of our leading citizens?"

"But I'm telling you—" Ethan begins.

The guard holds up one calloused hand. "Maybe you know

Vesonius, maybe you don't. For now you're coming with me."

"What about him?" Ethan sputters, pointing at Garius Chlorus.

"Bring your master to the jail tomorrow, Chlorus," Lucanus Honorius instructs him.

Chlorus bows, his eyes still leaking.

"Tomorrow," the guard repeats. "Don't make me find you."

The Roman soldier marches Ethan briskly through the city streets, the crowds parting to make way.

"Was that black pepper on the face of Garius Chlorus?" he asks.

"Yes," Ethan admits.

The Roman chuckles. "Don't worry, young man. Our justice is stern, but fair. If you haven't done anything wrong, you won't be in jail long."

But how long? In less than forty-eight hours, the final retrieval pulse will reach back from the future. After that, Ethan will be trapped in the past.

They approach a building that the guard identifies as the gladiator barracks. "The jail is in there," Lucanus tells him.

CONTINUE TO PAGE 59.

Releasing his grip on Ethan, Lucanus nods toward a low arch. "That way," he grunts. The building is lit by oil lamps hung from the high ceiling. They pass small rooms furnished with mattresses until the corridor ends at a closed door where another Roman guard dozes. As Lucanus Honorius approaches, the jail guard springs from the three legged stool and salutes.

"I thought you might be lonely, Capito. I've brought you a guest," Lucanus says, grinning.

"Name?" asks the sleepy guard, lifting one eyebrow.

Ethan gives his name to the guard.

"Another foreigner," he mutters, using a stylus to scratch the name on a wax pad. He glances at Lucanus Honorius and jerks his head toward the door. "Already got an African in there, dressed

like this one. Some strange name…" He studies the wax tablet. "Spencer Price."

Lucanus shakes his head. "I guess your African friend didn't take my advice, either."

Guard Capito removes a five-inch iron key from his belt and opens the heavy wooden door. He shoves Ethan into the room. Slamming the door behind him, the guard turns the key and calls out, "Welcome to Pompeii."

TURN TO PAGE 109.

ake works his way through the crowded street. People move aside, eyeing his clothing and admiring his height. Although Jake is a little tall for his age back in the 21st century, here he is taller than most of the adults he meets. He scans the bypassers for a glimpse of Ethan's father, but his eyes are drawn to the messages written on the white stone walls. Near a school, someone has written: I WAS WHIPPED FOR THE THIRD TIME. "Ha! You should have done your homework," Jake says, grinning. He passes a theater where one of the walls has been scribbled with MAY YOU SNEEZE SWEETLY. "That's too weird," Jake mutters. "Maybe I'll ask Spencer about it."

A little further he spots graffiti on a pillar: CELADUS IS THE

HEART THROB OF ALL THE GIRLS. Jake shakes his head. "The only girls who like Celadus," he mumbles, "are the ones who haven't met *me*."

TIME CRASHERS

MAKING A MARK

Writing on public walls was common in Pompeii. Scientists have found hundreds of writings like the ones Jake is reading. Of course, in our day writing on walls and doors is illegal and ugly. But here's a wall you can scribble on! Draw or write anything you like, but try to add at least one message about Jesus.

What are you waiting for? Go find a marker!

One graffiti message nails Jake's attention. A TROOP OF TEN GLADIATORS WILL FIGHT AT POMPEII. THERE WILL BE A BIG HUNT. Under the words is the painting of a bare footprint.

"Gladiators!" Jake exclaims. "A big hunt ... They must be bringing in wild animals. I'll bet that footprint is like a pointer."

He hurries down the street, keeping the city wall on his right. He passes a grassy area partially surrounded by pillars and covered porches. Young men splash and shout in a large pool. Beyond the green lawn, he spots the entrance to the stadium.

A broad-shouldered man with a pale scar running across his forehead leans in the doorway to the stadium. As Jake approaches, the man points with his chin and says, "Spectators enter down there.

This gate is for fighters."

The man pushes off from the wall and squeezes Jake's upper arm. "Not bad," he says. "And you're a big one. How about joining the games?"

"Really?" Jake asks.

"I can get you in," the man says, pointing a thumb at his own chest. "I'm Albus Aelius." He surveys Jake critically. "We'll have to get you armored up. Do you want to play the serious games or the warm-ups?"

Jake's main reason for entering the games is to make himself seen by a large number of people. If Ethan's dad is in Pompeii, he might be in the crowded arena. If Dr. Conway recognizes Jake, he'll find him after the games and they can return together to the 21st century. But should he fight in the warm-up games or the serious games? Does it make a difference?

IF YOU THINK JAKE SHOULD FIGHT IN THE WARM-UPS, TURN TO **PAGE 68.**

IF YOU THINK JAKE SHOULD FIGHT IN THE SERIOUS GAMES, TURN TO **PAGE 72.**

PRIDE: TAKE IT OR LEAVE IT?

Jake is proud to be a football player and athlete. He likes to compete, and he is glad for the gifts God has given him. Is there anything wrong with that? The Bible says, "Do not think of yourself more highly than you ought." (Romans 12:3) The Bible also says, "I praise you (God) because I am fearfully and wonderfully made; your works are wonderful." (Psalm 139:14)

The kind of pride that makes us thankful for our gifts and talents is a good thing; the kind of pride that makes us stuck-up or arrogant is a bad thing. How can we tell the difference? Unscramble each of these sentences and write it in the blank. Circle the statements that seem like healthy pride, and mark an X through the unhealthy ones.

FROM HELP I NEED DON'T ANYONE.

_____

HOW WHEN TO I I'M WRONG KNOW APOLOGIZE.

_____

LOVES JUST I WAY I BELIEVE THE ME AM GOD.

_____

TIME CRASHERS

A GAME WHEN I GET I LOSE ANGRY.

_____

OTHERS LIKE I SEE TO WELL DO.

_____

GOOD DOING I I'M THINGS ENJOY AT.

_____

SECOND THINK I LOSERS IS FOR PLACE.

_____

OTHERS TAKE FROM I CAN ADVICE.

_____

MY AM BLESSINGS I FOR THANKFUL.

_____

SEE ANSWERS ON PAGE 200.

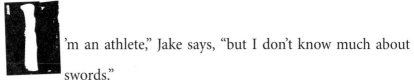'm an athlete," Jake says, "but I don't know much about swords."

Albus Aelius nods. "Fine. You'll be one of the lusorii, one of the fighters with a wooden sword. Don't worry. You'll learn fast."

Albus Aelius leads Jake into the gladiator quarters under the arena seats. In a few moments, Jake has replaced his jacket, vest, and shirt with a bronze helmet, a heavy, quilted sleeve worn on his right arm, a small round shield, and a blunt wooden sword. He also straps on greaves over his cargo pants, metal plates to protect shins and knees.

"Out you go," Albus Aelius orders Jake, pushing him through a tunnel that leads into bright sunlight.

"But what do I do?" yelps Jake.

"Fight!" Albus Aelius shouts. "Win!"

Jake emerges in the arena, surrounded by thousands of cheering people. Against one wall of the arena, on the same level as the fighters, are four cages. The athlete glimpses shadowy shapes in the cages, probably wild animals for the later fights. On the sandy floor of the arena, Jake turns to face another fighter, dressed much like himself, except that metal wings stick out from the top of his helmet. The gladiator hurls himself at Jake, screaming and waving his wooden sword. Waiting until the fighter is close, Jake sidesteps. As the enemy runs past, Jake smacks his butt with the wooden sword. The crowd roars.

"Hey, Winghead," Jake calls. "I'm over here. Try it again."

Winghead charges once more, sword held high. Under the protection of the helmet, Jake can't see much of his opponent's face, but he seems angry. Again, Jake waits until the last second, then drops to one knee and shoves his shield against the greaves of the other. Winghead flies over Jake's shoulder and thuds to the hot sand. Jake trots toward the fallen fighter to offer him a hand, but as Jake approaches, Winghead squeals with fear. "Don't hurt me! You win!" The frightened fighter flings away his sword and spreads his arms.

The crowd boos and hisses while a man wearing a scary horned mask and carrying a wooden mallet stalks toward the defeated fighter.

"Charon," someone shouts from the seats, "drag him away!"

The masked man, Charon, helps the loser stand and then chases him from the arena with his hammer. Jake lifts his arms to the crowd. The booing turns into cheers and applause.

When Jake returns to the gladiator rooms, Albus Aelius slaps him on the back. "Well done! You're not even sweating. Enough warming up. Do you want to fight with the big boys?"

 TURN TO PAGE 72.

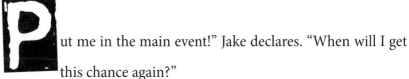

Put me in the main event!" Jake declares. "When will I get this chance again?"

"Good boy," Albus Aelius chuckles. "Let's get you into some real gear. But leave the leg-wrappings." The trainer nods at his slacks. "They make you stand out."

Jake puts on the scant armor provided by Albus Aelius. A broad belly band made of leather wraps around his waist. His left arm slides into a padded leather sleeve that reaches from armpit to wrist. On his left shoulder is a metal plate, a piece of armor that stands up like a fan.

"No helmet? No shield?" Jake asks.

"That would slow you down," Albus Aelius assures him. "What a retiarius needs is speed."

"Retiarius? Is that what kind of gladiator I'm supposed to be?"

"Yes, a net thrower," the older man explains. "Very popular with the crowd. Here are your weapons."

He hands Jake a short dagger to stick in his belly band, then a three-pointed pitchfork called a trident. Finally, he drapes over Jake's left shoulder a large net, neatly folded into a long web of cords.

"Where's my sword?" Jake demands.

"No sword," Albus Aelius shouts impatiently. "You are a net man."

A figure in a red knee-length tunic appears to usher Jake onto the field. He wears a horned mask with a horrible face.

"This is Charon," Albus Aelius explains. "He's here to make sure you don't change your mind about battling Hermiscus the secutor."

"Is Hermiscus any good?" Jake asks.

"Fifty fights and he's never been beaten," Albus Aelius says cheerfully. "But this could be his unlucky day."

Charon nudges Jake with a long-handled wooden mallet.

"But I don't know how to fight with a net," Jake protests as the masked man forces him through a dim tunnel leading into the arena.

"It's simple," Albus Aelius calls after him. "Tangle your enemy up and stab him. Then Charon drags the corpse off the field, everybody cheers and you're a hero."

"The corpse!?!?" Jake sputters. "I'm not about to kill somebody."

"No problem, boy," Charon says through his mask. "Then I'll

drag *your* body out of the stadium."

Laying the heavy mallet head on Jake's chest, Charon drives him from the tunnel and the time traveler stumbles backward into

the stadium. Glaring sun slants low from the west, turning the stadium into an oven. Heat rolls from the sandy ground as Jake sights his opponent. Hermiscus is a head taller than Jake and twice as wide as the Hulk. Although his chest is bare, the fighter's helmet, long shield, leg-guards, and sword have enough metal to make a sports car. Scars crisscross his chest and arms like a road map. An elaborate helmet hides his face; a metal plate tops the helmet like a fish fin. Jake imagines Hermiscus smiling wickedly behind the metal facemask, expecting a quick victory.

"I'm not going to make it easy for you," Jake promises under his breath. "No way I'm killing somebody for a stupid game, but I'm not lying down, either."

Jake realizes he can't out-battle this human fighting machine. The net is his best weapon. If he can tangle Hermiscus in the woven ropes, the giant won't be able to swing his sword. He'll be trapped like a bug in a cobweb. Holding the trident in his right hand, Jake opens the net in his left.

"Come on, little fly," Jake whispers.

But Hermiscus doesn't come any closer. Instead, he circles slowly, forcing Jake to turn. Too late, the time traveler realizes Hermiscus has maneuvered him into facing the sun. The glare stabs Jake's eyes as his foe lunges forward. Half-blinded, Jake hurls the net in desperation. It spins overhead, falling toward the gladiator, but Hermiscus snags it from the air with his sword point and flings it to the sandy earth. He plants heavy feet on top of the net.

Jake rushes forward, jabbing at Hermiscus with his trident. His only hope is to knock the fighter off-balance and grab his net for a second throw. With effortless motion, the gladiator thrusts his blade through the tines of the trident. He flips the three-pointed spear out of Jake's grip, then smashes the charging boy with his long, curved shield. Jake feels like he has come off the high dive face-first into a concrete driveway. Sliding down the shield like a broken egg on a brick wall, Jake slumps on the sand. Hermiscus looms over him.

Armed with the wooden hammer and wearing the horned mask, Charon scampers across the field. He faces the crowd and holds out one fist with his thumb pointed sideways. Slowly he turns his hand so the thumb points up. Should they let Jake live? The crowd unleashes a storm of booing and cursing.

Charon turns his thumb downward. Should the loser die? The blood-thirsty crowd roars its approval. "Kill him! Kill him!" echoes through the arena. Charon steps back while Hermiscus raises his razor-edged sword overhead. The spectators thunder and stamp their feet.

The sun filling his eyes, Jake fumbles in one of the pockets of his cargo pants. His fingers close on a flat rectangle about the size of a playing card.

"Hey, Goliath," Jake jeers. "Little David is about to kick your Roman rump."

He pulls out an unbreakable metal mirror. Catching the sun's rays, he flashes the blinding beams through the eyeholes of Hermiscus's helmet. The gladiator jerks his head to one side, then swings the deadly sword down.

But Jake is already rolling out of the sword's path. As the blade bites into the sand and Hermiscus is thrown off balance, Jake grabs the net with both hands. The gladiator's sandals are still planted on the net. As Jake jerks the strands, the net flies upward and Hermiscus overturns, hitting the earth like a falling tree. Faster than a heartbeat, Jake tosses the net over the struggling fighter. As Hermiscus tries to rise, Jake pushes him over again, tangling him in the tough, ropy web.

Recovering his trident, Jake leans over the helpless Hermiscus. The spectators leap to their feet, deafening Jake with their cheers. Charon lifts his fist and turns his thumb downward.

"Spill his blood!" the mob chants.

Charon gestures for Jake to finish Hermiscus.

"Let's see how you like it!" Jake shouts.

With the trident, Jake whips the wooden mallet from Charon's hands and tosses it away. Jabbing at the masked man, Jake hollers, "You look like the devil. Maybe you need a pitchfork."

Waving his hands in the air, the terrified Charon sprints across the arena. Jake follows behind, harmlessly poking his robed backside. Squealing like a pig, Charon races through the gladiator chambers and into the street.

Jake pauses only long enough to drop his trident and dagger. Pulling his clothes back on, he pushes past the gaping Albus Aelius toward the exit.

"Wait," Albus Aelius cries. "He's still alive. You can't leave yet."

In the doorway, Jake looks back, his blue eyes burning. "Who's going to stop me?"

Albus Aelius takes a frightened step backward.

"That's what I thought," Jake says. Without another word, he leaves the stadium. From the street, the roaring crowd sounds like the rumble of a coming storm. Without a backward glance, Jake strides angrily through the street, strollers scampering out of his way.

He doesn't get far before a commanding voice shouts, "Halt, foreigner, in the name of the Emperor!"

Jake turns and a Roman soldier grabs his arm in a granite grip. He forces Jake down the street.

"Where are you taking me?" Jake asks.

"Jail," the Roman grunts.

"For not killing a man?" Jake protests.

"For inciting a riot," the soldier informs him. "Don't talk again unless I ask you a question."

By the time the soldier hustles Jake to the jail, the athlete's anger has cooled. The Roman drags him into a squat building and down a long corridor. After scratching Jake's name on a wax tablet, a bored guard opens a heavy door, and pushes Jake inside.

In the dim cell, straw covers the floor and an oil lamp smolders on a stand. His eyes adjusting to the gloom, Jake hears a scratchy voice.

TURN TO **PAGE 111**.

TIME CRASHERS
CRASHERS TIME
TIME CRASHERS
CRASHERS TIME
CRASHERS
TIME CRASHERS · YOU DECIDE ·

Spencer watches his friends disappear and sets out on his own path through the crowded streets. A short man with a twisted leg hobbles toward Spencer, his dark eyes locked on the time traveler. From the corner of his eye, Spencer notices the limping man approaching. The man is probably harmless, but Spencer feels out of place in this strange city.

IF YOU THINK SPENCER SHOULD TALK TO THE MAN, CONTINUE TO PAGE 81.

IF YOU THINK SPENCER SHOULD SLIP AWAY FROM THE MAN, TURN TO PAGE 103.

Spencer waits for the man to hobble near and shows him the photo of Dr. Conway. The young genius explains that he is looking for this man.

The man with the bad leg shakes his head sadly. "I don't know him," he admits, "but I can help you find him. I will guide you through town—for a small fee."

"Sorry," Spencer says. "I don't have any money." He turns his pockets inside out for the man to inspect. "Not a single copper as," he adds, naming the tiniest Roman coin.

"Pompeii is harsh to those who have no coins," the man says with a shrug. He limps away, calling over his shoulder, "You have no money for me; I have no time for you."

But Spencer doesn't hear his parting words. One thought floods his mind: Pompeii! The ancient Roman city destroyed by a volcano. His gaze shifts to the mountain that rises in the distance. That must be Vesuvius.

"Don't panic," he mutters. "What are the odds we'd show up here on the day of the eruption?" But the warning bells are clanging again in his head. Didn't the guard at the gate say today was the Festival of Vulcan? Didn't the volcano erupt on the day after Vulcan's Feast?

Spencer notices another person staring at him in the crowded square, a girl with bright red hair.

"I overheard your conversation," the girl says. "No money at all?"

Spencer shakes his head, wondering what she wants. She has a pleasant round face and lively, intelligent eyes. She looks about fifteen years old. When she smiles, her blue-green eyes sparkle like stars.

"Have you eaten today?" the girl asks.

"Not really," Spencer says. Okay, he had a cookie a few hours ago, but technically that was a different day two thousand years in the future.

"I'm Monica," she says. She guides him toward the stall of a food seller.

"And I'm Spencer," he tells her, finding it easy to like this girl with her quick smile and sunny eyes.

From the food vendor, she picks up a cluster of fat grapes, a

piece of smoked fish, and a round, hard roll. She slides a coin to the seller and hands the food to Spencer.

"I can't repay you," Spencer says.

"No need," Monica assures him. "I believe in treating strangers with kindness."

As Spencer takes the food from her strong hands, he notices a fish tattooed on her forearm.

"Isn't that a Christian symbol?" he asks.

Monica's smiling face grows gray, and she flees into the crowd. Spencer tries to follow, but she disappears. He gobbles the food, turning in slow circles, trying to find the girl.

 CONTINUE TO **PAGE 85**.

As Spencer peers around, hoping to spot Monica's bright red hair, a charcoal drawing on the base of a fountain catches his eye. He stoops to study it.

"The ROTAS Square!" he breathes. "That proves there are Christians in the city. I wish I knew how to find them."

In the center of the fountain, the statue of a woman rises from the water. She cradles a pitcher in one arm, and her free hand points west. Spencer wonders if the pointing statue is a coincidence or if the stone finger shows the direction of the hidden Christians. Maybe they put the ROTAS Square here so the statue could serve as a signpost. Choosing a street in the direction of the pointing statue, Spencer moves toward the outskirts of the city.

The street narrows to an alley. Because he is watching closely,

Spencer spots the charcoal outline of a fish on the cobblestones outside a modest door. The fish is barely visible, easily erased when the meeting inside finishes. Spencer's heart pounds. He thinks he

 has found a secret church, a group of Jesus-followers from the early days when Christianity was small, undercover, and illegal.

He knocks on the door. A bearded man with shaggy eyebrows opens it a crack.

"I don't know you," he says to Spencer, starting to close the door.

"I am a friend of Monica," Spencer tells him, "and a servant of Jesus."

"Keep your voice down," the man says. He jerks Spencer inside, glances fearfully up and down the alley, and slams the door. The doorkeeper leads Spencer to an inner room where the window shutters are closed despite the heat of the day. Oil lamps brighten the dim space. A dozen people sit on cushions, encircling a short table that holds a loaf of bread and a wooden cup of wine.

Monica looks at Spencer in surprise.

"He followed me from the Forum," she says, her bright eyes fearful.

A frail man with a long, gray beard fixes wise, brown eyes on Spencer. "This is a private gathering, young man. Just a group of friends spending time together."

"I don't mean any harm," Spencer says. "I am a Christian, too."

"That is the sort of thing a spy might say," the old man observes in a steady voice.

Spencer shakes his head in frustration. "This is just like Paul trying to convince the Jerusalem leaders that he was really a Christian. They were afraid to believe him."

The gray-haired man inclines his head and asks, "Do you know Paul, young man?"

Spencer wonders what to say. If he pretends to know the apostle Paul, these Christians would trust him. They might know something about Ethan's dad. Would it be okay to tell a lie for a good cause?

 IF YOU THINK SPENCER SHOULD SAY HE KNOWS THE APOSTLE PAUL, TURN TO **PAGE 90**.

 IF YOU THINK SPENCER SHOULD ADMIT HE DOESN'T KNOW PAUL, TURN TO **PAGE 106**.

TOP SECRET!

In the early days of the church, the Roman Empire made it a crime to worship Jesus. Christians met for undercover worship and they used secret codes to let other Christians know where to gather. One of these codes is the ROTAS Square found in Pompeii. It looks like this:

R O T A S
O P E R A
T E N E T
A R E P O
S A T O R

No one knows exactly what it means, but the letters can be arranged into a cross like this:

The A and the O on the ends of the cross remind us that Jesus is the Alpha and the Omega, the beginning and end of everything. (You can look it up in Revelation 22:13.)

Pater Noster is Latin, the language of Pompeii. It means *our Father*. The words remind us that Jesus taught us to pray to our Father in heaven.

Congratulations! You've cracked the secret code! Aren't you glad you can be a Christian without hiding?

Do you know Paul of Tarsus?" the old man asks again.

In a way, Spencer does know Paul. After all, he has read Paul's letters in the New Testament and the story of Paul's life in the Acts of the Apostles. Even so, he feels a pang of guilt as he says to the old man, "Yes, I know the apostle Paul."

"You were young indeed when you knew him," the old man says gently. "Paul has been dead more than ten years."

Spencer's face burns with shame. At the same time, his thoughts race. If Paul died ten years before, the time travelers must have arrived in the late 70s AD, dangerously close to the time of the eruption.

"As I said," the old man tells Spencer, "you don't belong here."

Frightened eyes stare at Spencer. Monica's expression is disappointed and hurt.

"I'm sorry I lied," Spencer apologizes. "I don't expect you to trust me. But please tell me what year this is."

The elderly man looks puzzled. "It is the first year of Emperor Titus. He came to the throne only two months ago."

Spencer calculates the date in his head. The Feast of Vulcan in the first year of the reign of Emperor Titus: August 23, 79 AD. The day before Vesuvius completely destroyed Pompeii. In less than 24 hours, this city of 20,000 people will be wiped off the map.

"Pompeii is doomed!" Spencer shouts. "Tomorrow morning the mountain will bury your homes in ash and lava."

"More lies?" the gray-bearded man says sadly.

"Just listen," Spencer pleads. "Tomorrow morning in the fourth hour of the first watch, Mount Vesuvius will erupt. It will be a small explosion, and white ash will fall on the city like snow. When that happens, run away. The first eruption is only the beginning. More ash will come later, and finally surges of gas and lava. Pompeii will die. So will Herculaneum, Oplontis, and Boscoreale."

"Leave now," the old man tells Spencer.

"You have to believe me!" Spencer cries.

The elder rises slowly on skinny legs. "If you won't go," he says, "we will." He moves toward the door. The other Christians rise to follow. Monica passes Spencer with a disapproving glance.

"What I'm saying will come true," Spencer calls after them. "When it begins, remember what I told you. Run for the east. Don't take anything with you. Just run!"

 IF YOU THINK SPENCER SHOULD FOLLOW THE CHRISTIANS, TURN TO **PAGE 99.**

 IF YOU THINK SPENCER SHOULD TRY TO FIND JAKE AND ETHAN, CONTINUE TO **PAGE 93.**

After the Christian meeting scatters, Spencer stumbles through the crowded streets. He finds himself in the Forum and pushes through the crowds toward the Temple of Jupiter, but there is no sign of his friends as he climbs the steps. They may not return for hours. Neither of them understands the danger descending upon the city.

The young genius looks over the raucous crowd, knowing many of them will die soon. From the steps he shouts, "Run for your lives! Destruction is coming!"

Grinning faces turn in his direction.

"The mountain is going to erupt with fire and lava," Spencer declares.

"Which god told you this?" calls one of the spectators, laughing. "Vulcan is in charge of fire, and we've been celebrating his feast all day. Why would he be angry with us?"

"Bacchus, the god of wine, lives on top of Vesuvius," jeers another. "Maybe the boy found his message in a wine mug."

Laughter ripples through the crowd gathering at the foot of the temple steps.

"This is the truth," Spencer shouts, "not a message from your stupid, fake gods."

The smiles disappear, replaced by troubled expressions. For an instant, Spencer glimpses Monica watching him with wide, frightened eyes. Then the jostling crowd hides her.

"He insults the gods," cries a woman with pearls woven into her hair. "On the very steps of Jupiter's Temple!"

"He must be one of those Christ followers!" a fat man charges.

"Mocking the gods brings disaster," another man cries. "This African is a threat to our city!"

The angry mob surges toward Spencer.

TIME CRASHERS

 IF YOU THINK SPENCER SHOULD RUN, TURN TO **PAGE 96**.

 IF YOU THINK SPENCER SHOULD FACE THE CROWD, TURN TO **PAGE 100**.

Spencer dodges the clutching hands and sprints along the steps. As the stairs end, he plunges into the busy square, head ducked, weaving through the crowd. Angry cries ring behind him.

"Excuse me," he says, pushing through a knot of surprised people. "Sorry! Pardon me."

Suddenly, redheaded Monica grabs his arm.

"This way," she whispers urgently.

They wind through alleys and side streets. Just when Spencer believes they have escaped the angry mob, he and Monica turn a corner and come face to face with the angry fat man.

"Over here!" the heavy man shouts. "I've found him. There's a girl helping him!"

Seeing the danger from the hateful mob, Spencer turns on Monica and pushes her against a wall, pretending to be angry. "You led me right to them!" he shouts.

Monica blinks in confusion.

"Traitor!" Spencer shouts.

"Good job, girl," the fat man congratulates her, grabbing Spencer by the arm. As Spencer struggles, the thick-set man hails a Roman soldier on patrol.

"This African insulted our gods," the fat man says. "He almost started a riot."

"I don't care about religion," the guard says, "but I won't stand for rioting. You're coming with me, boy."

Monica watches as the guard arrests Spencer and takes him away, her expression worried.

After a quick march across town, the guard pushes Spencer down a long corridor in a barracks near the gladiator training school.

"Spencer Price. Disturbing the peace," the soldier tells the drowsy guard. "Let him cool off for a few days."

After scratching Spencer's name on a wax tablet, the jailer locks the boy in a small cell lit by a single oil lamp. Smelly straw covers the floor, choking Spencer and making it hard to breathe.

"You're all going to die!" Spencer yells at the thick door.

He uses his asthma inhaler and stretches out on the damp straw. "It's probably not a good idea to make fun of the gods other people believe in," he says aloud, "even if they are totally bogus and made up." Exhausted and aching from rough treatment, he closes his eyes and drifts off to sleep.

But his brief nap is interrupted when the guard Capito unlocks the door and shoves Ethan Conway into the musty room.

"Welcome to Pompeii," Capito snickers.

 TURN TO PAGE 109.

Desperate, Spencer runs into the street calling after the scattering Christians. He catches up with Monica.

"You're going to die if you stay here," he tells her. "Maybe God sent me to warn you."

"God doesn't send liars to carry his messages," Monica says, walking faster.

TURN TO **PAGE 93.**

Never mind your stone idols," Spencer shouts over the angry cries. "I'm trying to save you!"

"He is an enemy of religion. If we let him live, the gods will punish us!" a fat man roars. He is red faced, except for a white scar curving over one eye. He slaps Spencer and knocks him down. Clutching the boy's shirt-front, the enraged man drags him down the steps. He kicks Spencer and raises a fist, but a commanding voice breaks through the noise.

"Stop this rioting!" demands a Roman soldier.

The guard shoulders through the crowd and stands over the moaning Spencer. He has a short sword in his hand, face grim. He pokes the fat man with his sword. "What's going on?"

Flushed and sweating, the porky man points at Spencer. "He is predicting the downfall of our city and denying the gods."

The soldier eyes Spencer distastefully. "What's your name, boy?"

"Spencer Price," he says, swiping away the blood that leaks from his nose.

"I think he is a Christian," the heavy man says, making the name sound like a curse.

The guard points at the fat man and several others. "You, you, and you!" snaps the soldier. "Take him outside the city and deal with him." He raises his voice. "The rest of you get on with your business!"

The mob thins and the fat man drags Spencer to his feet.

"They're going to kill me," Spencer pleads.

"You should have thought of that before you mocked the gods, foreigner," the soldier growls.

Telling a lie has gotten Spencer in trouble, but another lie might save his life. Maybe he won't have to lie if he is careful with his words.

"Is this how you treat a Roman citizen?" Spencer asks the soldier.

The guard pales and fear floods his eyes. "Are you a Roman citizen?" the soldier asks.

But Spencer closes his eyes and lets his head fall limp, pretending to black out.

"No more fun!" shouts the soldier. "Roman citizens deserve Roman justice." He pokes the fat man again. "Take him to the jail."

Grumbling, the heavy man heaves Spencer over his shoulder and follows the guard through the noisy streets. The boy sneaks an occasional peek at the passing scenery, then closes his eyes tight as they enter a long, dimly-lit building. He is dumped on a pile of straw and locked in a small room. Through the heavy door he hears snatches of conversation.

"… Spencer Price. Claims to be a citizen…"

"… believe him?"

"…not my problem. Let Lucanus Honorius sort it out."

The moldy straw makes breathing hard, stirring Spencer's asthma. He pulls the inhaler from his pocket and sucks medicine into his lungs.

"Kicked out of church, beaten by a mob, and locked in a Roman jail with a volcanic eruption on the way," he mumbles. "I might as well rest up for whatever horrible thing is coming next." He closes his eyes again and is soon snoring softly.

He sleeps until the cell door flies open and Ethan Conway stumbles inside as the guard sneers, "Welcome to Pompeii."

 TURN TO **PAGE 109**.

Avoiding eye contact, Spencer moves away from the limping man, weaving hurriedly through the crowd. A few moments later, glancing over his shoulder, he sees no sign of the man with the twisted leg. As he worms through the busy Forum, a sweet smell tugs at Spencer, and he halts before a booth where a hawk-nosed man sells pastries. Pulling the picture from his pocket, he asks the cook if he has seen Ethan's father.

"I cannot help you find this man," the man sighs in disappointment. He suddenly brightens, "But I can help you find something good to eat. Maybe spira?" he asks, holding out a plate with twisted dough and honey. "Or globi, a ball of cheese and flour fried in olive oil?"

"My mouth is watering," Spencer admits, "but I have no money." He wishes he had eaten more of Miss Wigger's cookies back in the

21st century. His stomach is suddenly very empty.

"One of each," says a voice over his shoulder, "and extra honey, please."

Turning, Spencer sees a pretty red-haired girl with a round face and a smile like sunshine.

"Gladly, young miss!" the vendor says. He slides a plate of pastries toward her. She gives him two copper coins, then hands the plate to Spencer.

"A gift from Monica to a stranger," she says, smiling even more brightly.

"Thank you," Spencer says. "I don't mean to be rude, but what do I have to do for this food?"

"Just enjoy it," the girl says. "It's more blessed to give than to receive."

Spencer's eyes widen as the girl plunges into the crowd. She just quoted the words of Jesus. Monica must be a Christian!

Spencer pushes the pastries into his mouth, gobbling down the sweet dough, cheese, and honey. "Thankth! Itth wewy good," he sputters, mouth stuffed. He gives the plate back to the sharp-nosed man. He chases after the girl, but she is nowhere in sight.

 TURN TO **PAGE 85.**

No," Spencer admits, "I know stories about Paul, and I've read some of his letters. But I've never actually met the apostle."

"You are much too young to have known our dear Paul," the old man says gently. "After all, he died ten years ago. Maybe you are telling the truth about being a follower of the Way."

"Paul's been dead ten years?" Spencer asks uneasily. "What year is it, sir?"

"Do you come from so far away that you do not know the Roman calendar?" the gray-haired man asks.

"You wouldn't believe how far I've come," Spencer answers.

"It is the year 832 from the founding of Rome," the elderly man informs him.

The brainy boy squints into the distance, juggling numbers. His shoulders suddenly sag. "On my calendar, the year is 79 AD, and the Feast of Vulcan makes today August 23. This city will die tomorrow."

The Christians peer at one another in confusion.

"Tomorrow morning Mount Vesuvius will explode with fire and ash," Spencer continues. "Everyone who stays in Pompeii will be buried alive. Leave now while you can still get out of the city walls."

"How do you know this?" the leader asks. "Are you an angel?"

"Not an angel," Spencer says, "but I believe God sent me here to warn you."

A sudden pounding on the outer door booms through the house. "Open in the name of the Emperor!"

Everyone freezes with fear, except Spencer who flings open the door to confront the Roman guard outside.

"Are there Christians in this house?" the guard snarls.

"Just me," Spencer answers. "I thought a Christian church meets here, but I was wrong. Can you tell me where I might find other Christians in this city?"

"You are a Christian?" the guard asks, laying a hand on the hilt of his sword. "You admit this?"

"There is no Lord but Jesus!" Spencer declares. "He is the only Son of God."

"Treason!" the guard snaps. He drags Spencer into the street and pushes him violently. Over his shoulder he calls, "The rest of you go to your homes. Don't let me find you meeting together again!"

At sword point, the guard pushes his captive through the streets, shouting, "Make way! Move aside for the Emperor's justice!"

At the jail, a room in the barracks of the gladiators, Spencer's name is written on a wax tablet and he is locked into a small room stinking of rotted straw. Outside, the sun is setting and the shadowy cell is lit only with a flickering oil lamp.

"I think I just saved a whole congregation of Christians," he mutters, settling into the moldy hay. "I wonder who's going to save me?"

He snuggles into the straw, finds a comfortable position, and tries to sleep. Just as he is finally drifting off, the cell door bangs open and Ethan Conway is thrown into the straw.

"Welcome to Pompeii," the guard sneers.

CONTINUE TO **PAGE 109**.

Pompeii?" Ethan cries. "That guard says we're in Pompeii. Isn't that the town destroyed by the volcano?"

"That's right," agrees Spencer's familiar voice from a dim corner of the shadowy cell. "Do you want the good news or the bad news?"

"Let's have it all," Ethan sighs wearily.

"In about twelve hours Vesuvius is going to blow its top, and we're going to see the most amazing fireworks display of all time. That's the good news," Spencer explains. "The bad news is that we won't live long enough to see the end of the show." The young genius describes every horror the next few hours will hold.

When Spencer finishes, Ethan asks, "What do we do?"

"Get some sleep, if you can," Spencer advises. "There's a pot in the corner if you need a bathroom break. Believe me, it beats the public toilets. Stone seats so cold they send slaves to warm them up. And no toilet paper. Instead, they use sponges on sticks dipped in water—cold water!—followed by olive oil. All in all, the toilets are worse than the volcano."

Ethan hardly hears the rant about stone toilet seats. He buries his face in his hands. What has he gotten his friends into? There's no way he and Spencer will escape this cell in time to flee from the volcano. His only hope is that Jake will get back to the retrieval pulse. That hope dies suddenly as a key jiggles the lock and the door swings open. Jake Bradley stumbles inside and the door closes behind him.

"Oh, good," Spencer wheezes. "Is this the part where you rescue your buddies?"

"Ethan? Spence?" Jakes gasps. "You're in jail?"

Despite their desperate trouble, Ethan grins at the surprise in Jake's voice. "What would Pastor Calvin say if he knew three of his youth group were jailbirds?"

"I didn't do anything," Jake stammers.

"That's what they all say," Spencer assures him.

"We'll think of a way out," Jake says confidently. "They can't keep us in here forever."

"They don't need to," Spencer says. His voice is hoarse. He coughs deeply. When the coughing subsides, he uses his asthma inhaler.

"Save your breath, Spence," Ethan says. "I'll fill him in."

Spencer slumps in the corner while Jake settles in the moldy straw.

"Vesuvius is going ballistic," Ethan begins. "It's three hundred years since the last explosion, but we're here for the main event. The first eruption will be tomorrow morning around 10:00. That's a small one, a little smoke, the ground shakes a little, and ashes start to fall. Around 1:00 tomorrow afternoon the big eruption begins. Major quakes, falling buildings, panic in the streets, and stuff falling from the sky."

"What do we do?" Jake asks.

Spencer shrugs. "We die in a blaze of glory."

"Get your head in the game," Ethan snaps. "Do you think we left God behind in the 21st century? God brought us here for a reason, and God will get us home."

"We'll see," Spencer mutters weakly.

Ethan squeezes his arm in sympathy. "It's hard to keep your spirits up when you feel terrible. You concentrate on breathing. Jake and I will handle the believing."

After that, no one speaks. For a long time, the only sound in the cell is Spencer's labored breathing. Eventually they all sleep.

Much later, creaking hinges wake them. When the door opens, a different slant of light penetrates the cell.

"Looks like morning," Ethan yawns, stretching.

"I hope breakfast is on the way," Jake says.

"You!" The guard Capito gestures at Spencer. "You can go."

A red-haired girl hovers outside the door. "Spencer, are you well?"

Spencer blinks in the morning light. "Monica, is that you?"

"You gotta be kidding me," Jake says, planting his fists on his hips. "The book-worm has already found a girlfriend?"

"I got orders here," Capito says, waving a piece of parchment. "You're free, citizen."

Monica enters the cell and helps Spencer to his feet. "I found a friend to help you, a centurion named Lucanus Honorius."

"The guard we met at the gate?" Spencer asks in surprise.

Monica nods. "He's one of us," she whispers in his ear.

"The centurion is a—?" but Monica puts a finger on his lips and glances at Capito. She leads Spencer out of the cell.

Squaring his shoulders, Spencer says to the guard, "My friends leave with me."

"The orders say nothing about those two," Capito protests.

Monica edges behind the protesting guard and meets Spencer's eyes. Her expression contains a silent question.

 IF YOU THINK MONICA SHOULD TRY TO OVERPOWER THE GUARD, CONTINUE TO **PAGE 115**.

 IF YOU THINK MONICA SHOULD LET SPENCER TRY TO CONVINCE THE GUARD, TURN TO **PAGE 120**.

From behind the guard, Monica seizes the shoulder of his armor. With her other hand, she presses a sharp point against his neck.

"Don't reach for your sword," she says in a level voice. "My dagger is faster than your hand."

"Easy, easy," Capito pleads, his hands held high. "Don't do anything crazy."

"If you don't get crazy, I won't either," Monica assures him. "Take the key ring from your belt. Pitch it to Spencer."

Capito obeys, his face beaded with sweat.

After Jake and Ethan join them, Monica orders the guard, "Get in the cell."

Spencer slams and locks the cell door.

"It's lucky you carry a dagger," Jake says.

"I don't," Monica says. She holds up Capito's stylus, the pointed stick he uses to write on his wax tablet.

"The pen is mightier than the sword," Spencer says, laughing.

"What does that mean?" Monica asks.

"Nothing yet, but it will be a pretty cool quote in about 1800 years," Spencer admits.

The little band of runaways sprints through the long corridor and out of the building. In the distance a pillar of smoke rises from the peak of Vesuvius. Flurries of ash fall quietly from the sky, painting the city a pale gray.

"Now what?" Jake asks.

"I don't think we can escape before the eruption begins," Spencer explains.

"Didn't the volcano already blow?" Jake asks, brushing ash from his broad shoulders.

"That was the warm up," Spencer says grimly. "After the main event, rocks will be raining from the sky."

"So we keep moving," Ethan says.

The streets grow dim as clouds of smoke block the sun. Romans discuss the falling ash in fearful tones, eyes turned toward Vesuvius.

"Shouldn't we warn them?" Ethan asks.

"I tried that already," Spencer says, "and got mobbed."

A wagon rolls up the street, wheels crunching on ash. The driver pulls a fold of his toga over his silvery hair. The two horses move slowly, straining to pull the dozen people crouched in the wagon.

"You're leaving the city?" Ethan calls.

"What's that to you?" the driver replies suspiciously.

"Do you have room for one more?" Ethan asks.

"Maybe one," the man says, eyeing the foursome.

"Monica, you have to get out of Pompeii," Spencer says. "You can't go where we're going."

"Of course not," she says brightly. "You're angels and now you're going to fly away."

"We're not—"

"I don't need to know what you are," Monica interrupts. "But I have one question."

"Hurry," Spencer says, looking at the restless driver.

She leans close. "Rome hates us, all of us who follow Jesus. They've even killed some of us. What's going to happen?"

"It will get worse," Spencer tells her.

 TURN TO PAGE 142.

I'm a citizen, they're citizens!" Spencer snaps. Technically, the quick-thinking time traveler isn't lying. The boys are citizens, just not Romans. "Do you want Centurion Lucanus to come here in person to set you straight?"

"That won't be necessary," Capito says hurriedly. He waves the other boys from the cell. Capito brushes straw from their clothes and hair. "Unusual garments," the guard gushes, "but flattering. I was saying to a pal what striking outfits you wear."

Ethan nods toward Spencer and says coldly, "My friend needs a doctor. He has asthma."

"There is a healer right here in the barracks," says Capito, bowing stiffly. "We take care of our citizens." The guard scurries away, his rapid footsteps echoing down the hall.

A rumble like thunder explodes over the city. The floor shifts and tilts, before leveling again. All four kids fall, bouncing like ping-pong balls.

On hands and knees, Spencer pants, "We don't have time to wait for the doctor."

"We have to get across town and climb the slope toward the mountain to catch the retrieval pulse," Ethan reminds his friend. "You're in no shape to make it."

IF YOU THINK SPENCER SHOULD WAIT FOR THE DOCTOR, TURN TO **PAGE 122**.

IF YOU THINK SPENCER DOESN'T NEED THE DOCTOR, TURN TO **PAGE 144**.

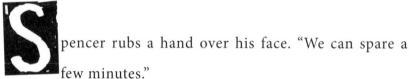

Spencer rubs a hand over his face. "We can spare a few minutes."

"You bet we can," Jake says. He pushes Spencer onto the stool. "If your asthma gets worse, you won't be able to talk. And how will we pass the time without your boring lectures on stuff nobody cares about?"

Monica takes Ethan aside. "Will he die?"

"He has a breathing disease," Ethan explains. "When he gets chilled or runs too far or breathes moldy air, his air passages fill up with mucus and less air gets through. He has medicine that helps, but this is a bad attack."

"You didn't answer me," Monica points out.

"I've seen him worse," Ethan says, "but we need to get home soon."

"Where is your home?" Monica asks, bright eyes glittering with curiosity.

"Home is far away," Ethan says carefully, "but it won't take us long to get there."

Monica snorts. "You are riddles wrapped in secrets."

The doctor, a jovial man with a red face, bustles in. The guard follows behind, carrying a tray of small bowls and bottles. The physician kneels beside Spencer. "Asthma, or so Capito tells me. Breathe deeply, young man. Again."

Spencer erupts in a fit of coughing.

"We'll fix you up," the healer says confidently. He snaps his finger, and Capito hands him a clay cup brimming with murky liquid. He presses the drug to Spencer's lips. The boy tries to protest, but the doctor has had practice giving medicine to unwilling patients. "Tastes awful. Best to drink it fast." Pinching Spencer's nose shut, the physician pours the smelly mixture down his throat.

"Good lad!" the doctor beams. "Henbane dulls the senses and relaxes the chest. You'll feel much better when you wake up."

"Henbane?" Spencer asks, already yawning. "Thass a bad idear. A verra, verra bad…"

His head slumps and his eyes close.

"Is he all right?" Ethan asks.

"He will be," the doctor responds. "I gave him a heavy dose.

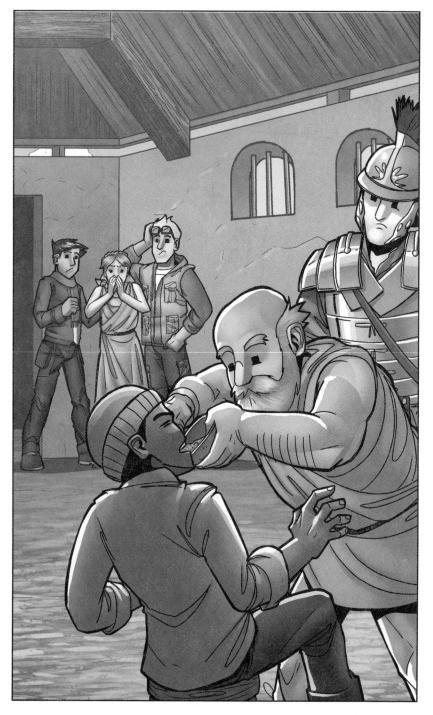

After ten or twelve hours of sleep, he'll be ready to climb Vesuvius!"

Ethan and Jake exchange worried looks.

The doctor dusts off his toga. "Let him rest. May you sneeze sweetly." He snaps his fingers again. "Capito, bring my drugs."

Ethan lightly slaps Spencer's face. "Spence!" he shouts. "Wake up, buddy!"

The only answer is a deep rumble. Walls tremble. Hunks of plaster drop from the ceiling.

"Outside!" Ethan shouts. He grabs Spencer's feet and Jake grips his shirt front. Together they lug the sleeping boy down the long corridor. Monica goes ahead of them, kicking aside fallen stones and other debris.

The rumbling grows louder, thundering across the city. Once outside, they move away from the barracks and lay Spencer on the bouncing ground. Along the street, pillars fall and red tiles cascade from rooftops. Cries of fear and pain mix with the roar of the quake. Behind them, a slab of wall breaks free from the barracks and crashes to the earth. A fruit seller's stall falls over, spilling red pomegranates into the street.

As the shaking slows, Monica points wordlessly at Vesuvius on the skyline. A tall trunk of black fumes sprays toward the heavens. Miles above the ground, the trunk opens into the terrifying shape of a deathly tree.

"Not good," Ethan says.

"Totally not good," Jake echoes.

"Without Spencer, we're in trouble," Ethan admits. "He's our answer man."

"We've got another twenty-four hours before the last removal bus, right?" Jake asks. "Let's get indoors and give Sleeping Brainy some time to wake up."

"People are grabbing their valuables and escaping," Monica says. "There must be lots of abandoned houses."

Draping Spencer over his shoulders in a fireman's carry, Jake hauls his friend through the throng of frightened people. Ash falls like warm snow from the darkening skies.

"I see two houses with their doors standing open, probably abandoned," Jake says. "That tall one and the other with only one floor."

"The big house," Monica shouts, running in that direction. "I always wanted to live in a two story home."

The house is abandoned. Scattered clothing and half-filled bags of food show that the owners left in a hurry. Jake lays Spencer in a bedroom and joins the others in the front room where Monica has scavenged a meal of dried fruit and brown bread.

After the meal, Monica rises. "I want to see what's going on."
She clutches a pillow on top of her
head and pushes through the door,
shoving aside several inches of ash
and rock on the porch. She is gone so
long that Ethan says to Jake, "Maybe
we should go after her."

Just then the door creaks open
and Monica returns, her clothing
gray with volcanic dust. She shakes the pillow clean and drops it
near the entrance.

"It's scary," she says, blue-green eyes wide. "Lightning is flashing
around Vesuvius, and fires burn on the slopes. The ash is falling even
faster. But I heard a rumor the Navy is coming to rescue us."

She folds her legs and flops next to Ethan.

"After the first small eruption this morning," Monica explains,
"someone sent a runner to the Navy commander at Misenum on the
other side of the bay. Commander Pliny is on the way with rescue ships."

Jake and Ethan exchange uneasy glances.

"If we get on a ship," Ethan says, "we'll never make it back in time
for the retrieval pulse. We'll be stranded here forever."

"Yeah," Jake nods, "but being stuck here alive is better than being stuck here dead. To catch the removal bus we have to travel toward the volcano. What will it be, chief?"

"Don't call me chief," Ethan says. He rubs his eyes, wondering what to do.

 IF YOU THINK THE BOYS AND MONICA SHOULD GO TO THE SEA FOR RESCUE, TURN TO **PAGE 151**.

 IF YOU THINK THE BOYS AND MONICA SHOULD STAY IN THE HOUSE, CONTINUE TO **PAGE 129**.

need time to think," Ethan says. "I'm trying to remember what Spencer told me and what we studied in World History."

"I must have been absent that day," Jake quips. "I've never heard of Pompeii."

"Fleeing citizens clog the streets," Monica agrees. "Let's rest for a while and then we'll decide. We'll make better time if the crowds have passed."

The short rest turns out to be longer than planned. One by one, the weary survivors nod off to sleep. Hours pass before Ethan awakens, rubbing bleary eyes. The oil lamp has burned out and the room is darker than a closet at midnight.

"Hey, Jake," Ethan calls.

"Hunh?" a drowsy voice answers.

"Wake up, buddy," Ethan says. "Do you have a light in one of those pockets?"

A moment later a flashlight beam plays around the room. Monica blinks in the light, shielding her eyes.

"We've slept too long," Ethan says, studying the face of his watch. "One way or another, we've got to escape from this city."

He tries the front door, but it feels nailed shut. Shoving his shoulder against the resisting wood, Ethan forces the door open a fraction of an inch. He looks through the crack and turns white-faced to the others.

"The ash is piled higher than the door," he tells them. "Pompeii is buried alive!"

ASHES! ASHES! ALL FALL DOWN!

The city of Pompeii was buried in a combination of pumice—volcanic rock—and ash. How deep was the ash and rock? Like drifts of snow, it was deeper in some places and shallower in others, but overall the city was buried in about seventeen feet of fallout from the eruption. To help imagine what that was like, find a crayon or a piece of chalk and a safe parking lot or sidewalk. First, lie down and measure your own height on the pavement, one mark by your feet and the other at the top of your head. Now draw yourself on the pavement. Next, use a yardstick or a tape measure to mark the pavement seventeen feet above the feet of your drawing.

Wow! Can you imagine that much ash falling on your neighborhood? Pompeii was luckier than some other towns nearby. The city of Herculaneum was buried in more than sixty feet of ash and pumice!

17 ft

5 ft

"U"pstairs," Ethan orders.

Jake ducks into the rear bedroom and returns with Spencer in his arms. He hands the flashlight to Ethan. They climb a marble stairway. From an open window they look across a city of ash-blanketed rooftops.

"It's still falling," Jake says in disbelief.

Ethan climbs through the window and drops a few feet to the crust of the ash. "It's solid enough to walk on," he calls.

Monica is the last one out. She straps a wet cloth over Spencer's face to keep him from inhaling dust and grit. As they creep across the gray landscape, Vesuvius belches flames. Lightning crackles around its summit. Otherwise, all is darkness. Heavy smoke has turned the summer day into night.

"My home town has become a city of death," Monica says in a broken voice.

As they circle a pile of rubble, a pitiful animal cry echoes through the dark. Drawing closer, Jake's flashlight shows two horses, one red and one black, buried to the shoulders in the ash. Their eyes are wild and fearful, their pelts speckled with sweaty lather. Behind the horses, shards of a broken wagon jut through the cinders.

"Maybe a wall fell on the cart and trapped them," Ethan says, crouching near the animals. "Now the ash is swallowing them."

"Not if I can help it," Jake vows.

He lays Spencer down and wrenches a piece of the shattered wagon free from the cinders. He pitches the jagged board to Ethan and pries another loose. As the boys hack at the ash, Monica speaks softly to the horses. When most of the ash is cleared, Jake opens his Scout knife and saws at the leather straps tying the horses to the buried wagon. Gripping the harness, he coaxes the black horse from the pit. Snorting fiercely, the animal clambers from the hole. Ethan helps the red horse free.

The black stallion approaches uneasily and nuzzles Jake's arm. The red mare dips her head, nickering softly, and Monica brushes ash from the muscled neck.

"One horse to carry Monica away from Vesuvius," Ethan says, "and one horse to carry Spencer toward Vesuvius."

"I can't go with you?" Monica asks.

Ethan shakes his head firmly. "You belong here, not where we're going."

"Who are you?" she asks. "You say strange things. You have a shiny stick." She nods at Jake's flashlight.

"God sent us to help you get out of Pompeii," Ethan tells her, "and God sent you to help us escape."

"So we're angels to each other." Monica clutches the mare's mane and pulls herself onto its back. "I'll take the redhead," she says, grinning.

"Take the shiny stick, too," Jake offers. He knows that nothing can be left in the past. When Jake gets home, the flashlight will return with him, appearing in his pocket.

"Thank you!" The red mane in one hand, the flashlight in the other, Monica gives them a parting smile that lights up the dark landscape.

"North and east," Ethan reminds her.

"Tell Spencer to pray for me," she calls as the horse canters away.

"Have you enjoyed your Pompeii vacation?" Ethan jokes as he and Jake wrestle Spencer onto the broad back of the stallion.

The unconscious boy hangs over the horse, head dangling on one side and feet on the other.

"I was hoping for better weather," Jake says, "and some beach time."

"Too bad you didn't get to soak up any rays," Ethan sympathizes. "Maybe you'll still get to soak up some lava."

Jake ties together some of the leather straps from the horse's harness and loops it around the animal's neck. He leads it west toward the rumbling mountain. Spencer stirs, mumbles, and falls back into a sound sleep.

Jake shakes his head. "He's dreaming about getting locked in a bookstore. Nothing to do except read all night. What a nightmare!" Jake says with a shudder.

"Unless it was a comic book store," Ethan kids him.

"That's my kind of dream," Jake says. "But after this trip, the Human Torch isn't my favorite hero anymore. Hmmm… That gives me an idea."

The athlete fumbles in his jacket and finds a roadside emergency flare. He peels the cap off and strikes one end against a stone. The flare sputters to life, throwing bright light and long shadows.

"Oh, good," Ethan chuckles. "More fire and smoke."

They hike over the weird terrain, using the flare to avoid sinkholes and soft spots in the crust. Here and there the heads of statues poke from the ashes.

"Do you think we're the last ones in the city?" Jake asks.

"I doubt it," Ethan guesses. "There must be people hiding in homes or trapped in basements."

They trudge along in the daytime darkness, ash crunching underfoot, moving step by step toward the place they first appeared on the outskirts of town.

"When they dug this place up," Ethan says. "I mean when they will dig this place up in the future, Spencer told me they'll find about two thousand corpses buried in the ashes."

"Wow," Jake says, whistling between his teeth. "We're probably walking on top of people right now, like a graveyard."

"A graveyard at midnight, covered with creepy gray snow," Ethan adds.

"Spencer is missing the fun," Jake says as they clamber through a break in the city wall.

After they leave the city behind, the layer of ashes thins.

"That's weird," Ethan says. "Wouldn't you expect to find more ashes as we get closer to Vesuvius? I guess the ashes go high into the sky, and as they come down the wind blows them away from the eruption."

"Black Beauty is getting nervous," Jake points out. The horse stops, pawing at the ground. Jake tugs on the strap, but the stallion won't budge.

"He knows there's danger ahead," Ethan decides.

"Basically he's smarter than us, right?" Jake removes the leather cord and slides Spencer onto his own shoulders.

"Horse sense," Ethan says.

"Thanks, buddy," Jake tells the stallion. He slaps Black Beauty on the rear and the horse gallops away.

"We're close," Ethan says, pointing the way with the flare.

"Good," Jake pants. "For a little guy, Spencer weighs a lot."

"Maybe it's the fifty pounds of brains crammed into his head," Ethan suggests. "As soon as we get home, he'll be wide awake. The henbane drug will be left behind here in the past and he'll be his old self."

At last, they reach the olive grove where they first appeared. At least, they think it's the same olive grove. Although the ash isn't more than six inches deep here, fires have spread across the slopes and foothills of Vesuvius, torching grapevines, consuming gardens, and burning the olive trees to twisted black stumps.

"Everything looks different," Jake says, worry in his voice. "Is this the right bunch of trees?"

"Absolutely," Ethan says, trying to sound certain. If it's not the right grove, what can they do? Wait for a pulse that isn't coming here? Move from one bunch of burnt trunks to another, hoping to stumble on the right place? How long do they have before the big eruption?

"Okay," Jake says, "but how do we find the right tree? My orange X is buried under ash. We can't sweep around every stump."

"Spencer came up with a way to remember which tree will take

us home," Ethan reminds him.

"Let me think," Jake says, forehead furrowed. "It was Mark 5:19! Count five trees to the east, then nineteen trees to the north. No, wait. Maybe it was Mark 19:5. That would be nineteen trees to the east and five to the north."

"Those are completely different trees," Ethan points out. "We need to remember that verse."

"It was something about going home," Jake says. "Can you look it up?"

"Remember how time travel messed up my palm tablet on the last trip?" Ethan asks. "So this time I brought a real Bible instead."

"Yay! We're saved! Look up both verses and see which one talks about going home!" Jake shouts.

"I lost my Bible," Ethan admits. "I think it fell out of my pocket in the jail."

Jake squints, staring hard at nothing. "Okay, it's coming back to me. It's definitely Mark 19:5."

"I'm pretty sure it's Mark 5:19," Ethan argues.

No fair looking back at the beginning of the book!

 IF YOU THINK THE VERSE IS MARK 19:5, TURN TO **PAGE 187**.

 IF YOU THINK THE VERSE IS MARK 5:19, TURN TO **PAGE 191**.

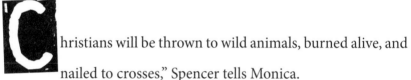

Christians will be thrown to wild animals, burned alive, and nailed to crosses," Spencer tells Monica.

"Will Rome win?" Monica whispers. "Will they destroy the church?"

"In four hundred years, the Roman Empire will fall down like these broken buildings," Spencer assures her. "But the church of Jesus will survive and spread through the whole world."

Monica nods. "I won't see you again, will I?"

Spencer grins. "Christians always see each other again."

Now Monica smiles too, a sunny smile that lights her sea-colored eyes.

"We're leaving," the old man warns, "with or without you."

Monica scrambles onto the seat beside the driver.

"Go north and east," Spencer calls to the old man. "Get across the Sarno River before the bridge falls. Don't go to the sea. Do you understand?"

"He is a prophet," Monica assures the driver.

The old man scratches his head. "Who am I to argue with the gods?"

"I hope she makes it," Spencer says as the wagon clatters away.

"I hope we make it, too," Ethan says, hunching against the volcanic fallout.

 TURN TO PAGE 162.

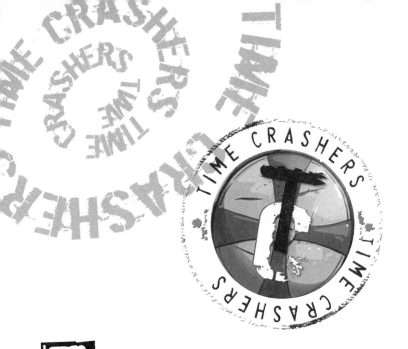

Time is not our friend," Spencer insists in a labored voice. "I don't have time to wait around for an ancient Roman quack who wants to cure my asthma by sticking leeches on my chest."

"Yuchhh!" Jake says. "Leeches? The things that drink blood?"

"You can handle this?" Ethan asks his friend.

Spencer nods. "Let's see. There's Option A: Breathe hard. Or Option B: Take a lava bath. Not a hard choice."

They hurry down the corridor and into the bright street where flurries of ash fall like light snow. Puzzled pedestrians stroll along the avenue, glancing at the sky curiously.

"Monica, we have to get you out of Pompeii," Spencer says earnestly. "Do you want to grab any of your friends?"

"All my friends are in the…" She drops her voice to a whisper.

"…the church. I convinced them to trust you. They are already on their way out of this wicked city."

Spencer nods in satisfaction.

"Where shall we go?" Monica asks. "The harbor?"

"No!" Spencer snaps. "There is only death waiting at the sea. Commander Pliny will try to bring rescue boats to the shore, but the waves will be too rough for him to land. He won't be able to save anyone. Instead, he'll die himself."

"Then where?" Monica asks.

"Across the river," Spencer declares. "Take us to the Sarno Gate by the shortest route."

She pauses, considering the route. "Right or left?" she wonders aloud.

Monica turns right and leads them through the stricken city, keeping to the middle of the streets to avoid falling walls. The day grows darker as more smoke fills the sky, and the fall of pebbles and ash is a constant torment. Monica finds a discarded spear and uses it as a staff to steady her pace over the wreckage. Everyone is panting from exertion, especially Spencer.

"Not much further," Monica calls, stopping for a rest.

A faint breeze stirs the ashes at their feet, then subsides. For a moment the city is eerily silent. In the stillness, a low snarl pierces the dim air. Turning slowly, the exhausted kids raise their eyes to a nearby window in a leaning wall. Crouched on the sill is a growling leopard, green eyes fiery with rage. The cat's lips curl back, revealing teeth sharper than knives.

"He must have escaped from the stadium," Jake whispers. "I saw animal cages there."

"Make him think we're too big to handle," Spencer says in a measured voice. "Remember how we made a giant in gym class?"

Moving at turtle speed, Jake kneels in the street while Ethan climbs on his shoulders. Spencer climbs on top of Ethan and Jake staggers upright.

"Spread your arms," Spencer suggests. "Look big!"

The growling cat studies the three-person giant. The muscles in his hind-legs bunch. With a blood-freezing snarl he leaps at the boys, clawed paws extended and teeth bared.

But the ferocious leopard never reaches its prey. A spear slices the air and the point stabs into the cat's belly. The beast screeches, shivers, and falls unmoving to the littered pavement inches in front of Jake. Monica stands to one side, arm still extended from the throw.

"Poor thing," she says, wetness on her cheeks and anger in her voice. "They starve and beat the animals to make them fierce for the games. This wicked city deserves to burn."

"Look big?" Jake asks Spencer. "That's your best shot?"

"That's what the survival book said," Spencer replies defensively.

"I guess the leopard didn't read the book," Jake decides.

As they resume their journey toward the Sarno Gate, Ethan asks Monica, "Where did you learn to throw a spear?"

"I used to practice with my brothers," she says, a note of grief in her voice. "They were gladiators. After they both died in the games, I wanted more from life than killing or being killed. I began to follow Jesus."

The Sarno Gate is in sight when the next quake strikes. Deafening sounds crack the air: grinding mortar, falling stones, screams of fear, and the thunder of Vesuvius. Beneath their feet, the ground lurches and rolls, while overhead flocks of squawking seabirds flee the city. The statue of a goddess near the gate falls face down, and her head bounces across the pavement. Cracks zigzag across the pavement like lightning. When the quake stops, wailing echoes in the streets.

The foursome press through weeping people, some of them bloody. They scramble over a spill of broken marble to the gate.

Spencer faces Monica, squeezing her arms. "Thanks for getting us out of jail."

"Come with me?" Monica asks.

"We don't belong here," Spencer tells her.

"No, you don't. But I'm glad you came." Monica hugs Spencer. "God bless you," she says. Stepping back, she adds, "All of you."

"And you, too, Red," Jake says. "Who knows how many centuries it will take before Spencer finds another girlfriend?"

Monica giggles and hurries out the gate toward the Sarno River. She waves once and disappears around the corner of the wall.

TURN TO **PAGE 162**.

"We could go to the sea coast to check things out," Ethan says uncertainly. "We'd still have time to get back for the last Pulse home if we decided not to get on a ship. We could put Monica on a boat, at least."

"That's settled," Jake says, getting up from the cushions. "Doing nothing is driving me bonkers."

Ethan finds two long pieces of wood and ties purple drapes between them to create a stretcher for Spencer.

"He's breathing better," Jake admits. "Maybe that shin pain is working."

"Henbane," Ethan corrects him with a grin. "Until Spence wakes up, I'll have to keep you straight."

TIME CRASHERS

The trip to the seaside is exhausting. The ash and cinders are inches deep, hidden stones making it easy to stumble or twist an ankle. Clouds of smoke block the  sunlight, creating a land of always-night in the middle of the day. They are soon coughing in the thick air. Falling grit clings to their sweaty skin, painting their faces. By the time they reach the bay, several more inches of ash lie on the ground.

Clusters of desperate Romans huddle on the beach. Some hold torches, others sit in forlorn weariness.

"There's a ship!" someone shouts. "I can see the lanterns on the rigging."

The ship labors in the quake-churned waters. A thick scum of ash and pumice bobs on the angry waves. Sailing through the muck is like forcing the ship through molasses.

"They're turning back!" a woman screams. "They are leaving us to die!"

Across the dark beach, sobs and curses float in the heavy air.

"Any ideas, captain?" Jake asks.

"Don't call me captain." Ethan chews his lower lip and rubs gritty sweat from his eyes. "While we were in the cell, I think Spencer said something about heading north-east."

 IF YOU THINK MONICA AND THE BOYS SHOULD WAIT ON THE BEACH, CONTINUE TO **PAGE 155**.

 IF YOU THINK THEY SHOULD HEAD NORTH-EAST, TURN TO **PAGE 158**.

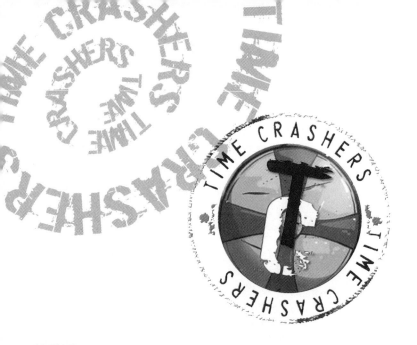

W e'll wait a while and see if the waves die down," Ethan suggests. "Whatever we decide to do about the retrieval pulse, I think the ship is Monica's best hope."

"I could use a rest anyway," Jake agrees.

They sit on the ashy beach, brushing dust and cinders from the snoring Spencer.

"He's going to hate missing the fun," Jake says.

"This is fun?" Monica asks.

"Shhh!" Ethan hushes the others.

The sound of rushing water fills the air, like dishwater swirling down the drain. The waves are rolling away from the shore, exposing the ocean bottom as if someone pulled a plug in the floor of the sea.

"That's weird," Ethan begins, then slaps a palm against his dusty forehead. "Tsunami! We gotta get out of here!"

The boys grab Spencer's stretcher and run desperately toward the mainland. Monica chases them, shouting, "What's a tsunami?"

"A Godzilla wave," Ethan pants. "The quake shakes the ocean floor. Water rolls out, then surges back."

In the darkness, Ethan stumbles and falls. Spencer spills from the stretcher and sprawls on the ashy sand. Monica rolls the sleeping boy back onto the fabric. Ethan grabs the handles and lifts the weight, but Jake is staring at the dark sea.

"Oh, man," Jake says.

A wall of water four stories high thunders onto the beach, burying screaming people, crushing everything in its path.

Jake throws himself on top of Spencer as the tidal wave strikes like a runaway train. In a murderous swirl of water, the beach is scoured clean of people and baggage. Thunder rumbles over the raging sea. No one emerges from the ash-blanketed waters. A few hours later, two wooden poles tangled with waterlogged draperies wash up on the silent shore. Falling cinders soon bury the purple cloth.

THE END

YOU DON'T LIKE THIS ENDING?

DO YOU WISH THE TIME CRASHERS HAD MADE OTHER CHOICES? GOOD NEWS! YOU HAVE A TIME MACHINE. GO BACK AND DO IT DIFFERENTLY. THE FINAL ENDING IS UP TO YOU!

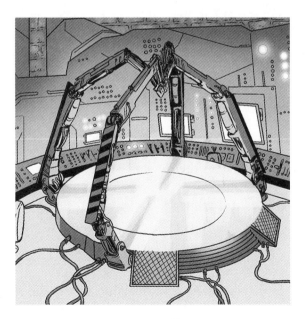

We can't wait on someone else to save us," Ethan decides.

They raise the stretcher and move away from the beach. As the sound of waves falls behind them, Monica says, "We have to cross the Sarno River if we travel east."

"Is there a bridge?" Ethan asks. When Monica nods, he adds, "Take us there."

The traveling is slower than before. More fallout blankets the ground, rising halfway to their knees. The path is uphill, each step a struggle. The river winds among vineyards and olive groves in a shallow valley. Trees and vines sag under the weight of ash. A thick scum of fallout chokes the surface of the river. Pumice, or volcanic rock, is lightweight and floats on water. The river moves swiftly toward the bay, the gray blanket on top of the water heaving.

A dim shape appears ahead. Moments later they reach the bridge. The stone arch spans the racing river, but quakes have damaged the structure. Holes gape where stones have shaken loose and tumbled into the water below.

"Is there another bridge?" Ethan asks Monica.

"Not close enough for us."

"No way we can swim," Jake says. "Not with that current and the muck on top."

"One at a time," Ethan says. "Jake, you're first."

The athlete frowns. "What about Sleeping Brainy?"

"I'll bring Spencer," Ethan says. Jake argues, but Ethan cuts him off. "Weight makes a difference. Spencer on my shoulders is lighter than Spencer on yours. You go first. If you make it across, we know it's safe for Monica. Then I'll bring up the rear."

Reluctantly, Jake tiptoes onto the bridge. Placing his feet with care, he picks his way across the broken stones. Ethan and Monica breathe a sigh of relief when he reaches the other side.

"Your turn, Monica," Ethan tells her. The redhead follows Jake's path, stepping in his footprints in the ash. When she is across, Ethan heaves Spencer over his shoulder, and sets out. Through gaps in the rock, the river swirls below. Twice he stumbles on the uneven stones but catches himself and continues. In the middle of the bridge, a ragged grinding sound freezes his heart. The bridge trembles. Stone slabs tilt under his feet. Suddenly Ethan and Spencer plunge toward the racing current. Splashing through the blanket of ash, the boys disappear beneath the cold water.

"Ethan!" Jake shouts. From the bank he cuts through the scum in a clean dive.

Monica runs along the bank, kicking through the snowy ashes. She calls the names of her strange friends. The Sarno is a dangerous river, a place no one swims. In the dark, with the choking ashes on the surface and the deadly current beneath …

She plods downstream, watching for wet figures to pull themselves onto the bank. After half a mile, she turns away. With tears tracking her dusty face, she trudges from the valley, leaving death and destruction behind.

THE END

YOU DON'T LIKE THIS ENDING?

DO YOU WISH THE TIME CRASHERS HAD MADE OTHER CHOICES? GOOD NEWS! YOU HAVE A TIME MACHINE. GO BACK AND DO IT DIFFERENTLY. THE FINAL ENDING IS UP TO YOU!

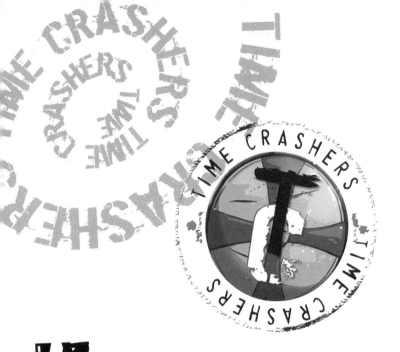

Another quake seizes the city. As if in slow motion, a house across the street tumbles to the ground, an avalanche of bricks and mortar. Vesuvius belches an orange geyser into the sky. The shaking ends, but now bits of stone and pumice are mixed with the falling ash. Spencer steps into a doorway to escape the pummeling ash. "We have to cross the city to the Vesuvius Gate," he explains. "That's the way we came into Pompeii, the gate closest to the retrieval pulse."

"Let's beat feet," says Jake.

"Not yet," Ethan says, pointing to a nearby house. A dog is chained near the open door. The animal cringes, eyes terrified.

"A Laconian hound," Spencer says impatiently. "The Romans imported them from Greece. So what? We can't stop for every stray in the city."

"We can stop for this one," Ethan says.

LOVE YOUR NEIGHBOR'S PET?

Do you think the boys should take time to help an animal when there is so much danger? There is a verse in the Bible that might make up your mind. To read the verse, scratch out every B, P, K, W, and J from the message. (If you get stuck, you can look up the verse in Proverbs 12:10.)

AWRJBIGKPHTJPEKOBUPSMWAJBN
PCAKRWESBFOJPRTBHEPNEKEWJBD
SOKFBHWPISABJNIPMKWAL.

_____

_____

_____

_____

_____

SEE ANSWERS ON PAGE 200.

The dog wags his tail hopefully as the time travelers kneel beside him. He is a large tan dog, his head, chest, and legs splashed with white. His ears stand upright on a small head set on a long neck. He licks Ethan's fingers while Jake studies the chain on his collar.

"When scientists dug up the city of Pompeii in the 1800s they found the remains of a dog who was left chained," Spencer says. "The animal was curled in a ball, two legs sticking into the air. As the ash piled up, the dog kept climbing higher until it ran out of chain. Then the ashes smothered it inch by inch."

"Yeah, Professor?" Jake asks. "What's your point?"

"I was wrong," Spencer admits. "No matter how little time we have, I don't want to be a person who leaves a helpless animal to die."

"You'd have changed your mind," Ethan says, "before we covered half a block."

The wriggling dog scampers around their feet.

"Spencer just admitted he was wrong about something," Jake declares. "Let's carve it on a wall so scientists in the future can put it in a museum."

"We can't wait here while you learn the alphabet, Jake," Spencer replies. "For now we need to decide whether we should stick to the main avenues or move to the alleys."

 IF YOU THINK THE TIME CRASHERS SHOULD TRAVEL ON MAJOR STREETS, CONTINUE TO **PAGE 167**.

 IF YOU THINK THE TIME CRASHERS SHOULD TRAVEL ON SIDE STREETS, TURN TO **PAGE 171**.

We can't afford to get lost," Jake says. "Let's plow through the main streets. I can push as hard as anybody."

The crowds are frantic, but Jake's strength makes progress easier. They travel toward the volcano, while everyone else surges in the opposite direction. Jake lowers his head. He muscles through the throng like a man wading upstream, Ethan and Spencer following. The dog keeps pace, weaving between legs.

"What kind of dog did you say this is?" Ethan asks.

"Laconian," Spencer says. "A breed known for fighting and hunting. They have a great sense of smell."

"Laconian? We'll call him Coney," Ethan decides.

They pass many blocks without difficulty, but suddenly a fat man points at them and yells, "These are the foreigners who came here to insult our gods!" A puckered scar angles over his right eye. "That's why Vesuvius threatens us."

"Let us through!" Ethan shouts.

"Kill them!" a gray-haired woman squeals. "Sacrifice them to the gods!"

"Bring it on!" Jake raises his fists.

The boys huddle back to back, facing the mob. But before the first blow lands, Coney lowers his haunches and growls viciously. He circles the boys, teeth bared, and the crowd retreats.

"Gutless!" Jake calls. "Two hundred against four, and you chicken out?"

"Leave them to the gods," the fat man mumbles, waddling away. "It's not our responsibility."

"It's good thing we saved the dog, huh?" Jake says out of the corner of his mouth to Spencer.

The river of people begins to flow again, swirling past the boys as if they are an island in a stream. Jake drops to his knees and hugs the dog.

"Coney, you are the man!" Jake exclaims.

"Technically a man is Homo sapiens and Coney is Canis lupus familiaris, a completely different species," Spencer points out.

Tugging playfully on the dog's ears, Jake says, "Do you want to come home with us, buddy? We'll leave Professor Egghead behind, and you can take his place. You're tougher than him and you don't

talk, so we'll swap you. You're gonna love the 21st century. Television. Chewy treats. Potato chips."

"It'll never work," Spencer says. "He doesn't speak English."

The Time Crashers press on. The nearer they get to the Vesuvius Gate, the thinner the crowd. The ash and pumice fall fiercely, piling up several inches per hour. Already the fallout blankets the pavement higher than their ankles. They trudge through it like they are walking in autumn leaves.

 TURN TO **PAGE 175**.

e'll be going against the traffic," Spencer points out. "We'll make better time on the back streets."

On the narrow side streets the crowds thin, but the rain of ash thickens. Heavy ashes, small pebbles, and fragments of pumice pelt the boys, piling up like snow. The dog trots happily through the ash at their feet.

"He's a Laconian?" Ethan asks. "Let's call him Coney."

"The Laconian hounds were famous as fighters and hunters," Spencer says. "They track by smell."

The boys travel for blocks, passing few people. At a narrow place, they pick their way over a pile of rubble. As they reach the other side of the fallen bricks, a thick-set man emerges from a doorway, a bag

in hand. His square face turns toward the boys, and Ethan shouts, "Garius Chlorus!"

The man flinches, cowering at the sound of his name. When his eyes fall on Ethan, he sneers and draws a dagger from his tunic.

"You know this man?" Jake asks.

"His name is Liarus Thiefus Jerkus," Ethan snarls.

"He's looting houses," Spencer says, pointing to the lumpy bag.

Chlorus smirks. "If they don't care about their jewelry and silver cups, why shouldn't I have them?"

"Get out of the city," Spencer says. "Stay here and you'll be a very rich dead man."

"Says you," Garius Chlorus answers. He shakes the bag. "This is just a start. I won't leave until I have a wagon loaded with treasure."

Ethan bunches his fists. "We have things to settle, Garius Chlorus."

"Don't bother," Spencer says. "In eighteen centuries they'll dig up a skeleton surrounded by coins and jewels. People will think he was killed by Vesuvius, but they'll be wrong. He was killed by greed."

The looter shakes his head. "I'll never take orders again. Slaves will feed me from a golden plate."

Dagger extended, Garius Chlorus backs away and disappears into an alley. The boys hear coins jingling as he scampers away.

"Is he really going to die?" Ethan asks.

"It's hard to run dragging a hundred pounds of metal," Jake says.

"The excavators will find the bodies of many who tried to carry wealth out of Pompeii," Spencer says. "Would you be surprised if Garius Chlorus were one of them?"

The boys hike on, feeling greater urgency as the ash deepens. "How high will the ashes pile up?" Jake asks.

"At this rate, about six inches per hour," Spencer says. "By the time the eruption finishes, fifteen to twenty feet of volcanic fallout will bury Pompeii."

Trying to imagine a whole city smothered by ashes, the boys move on in silence.

■ ■

Ashes and smoke swallow the daylight. The sun shines behind the billows of smoke, but Pompeii is dark as night. As they reach the gate, they spot a Roman soldier on guard duty holding a sputtering torch.

"Lucanus Honorius!" Ethan calls in surprise. "Get out of the city!"

"I serve the Emperor," the guard says proudly. "I have received no orders to leave my post."

"Pompeii is doomed," Spencer tells him. "So are you if you stay."

"Then I will die with the honor befitting my rank," Lucanus Honorius tells him.

"You don't understand!" Jake blurts.

"No, you don't understand," Lucanus Honorius says. With the toe of his heavy sandal, he traces the outline of a fish in the ash at his feet.

"The secret code for Christ!" Spencer exclaims.

"I'm not afraid to die doing my duty," The Roman says, handing a torch to Jake. "This gate leads to Vesuvius."

Ethan nods. "We know where we're going."

"Then you are wiser than most," the Roman says, smiling. "God give you a safe homecoming."

"You, too," Jake says, blinking wet eyes.

As the boys pass through the gate in the storm of pumice, Jake glances back at the guard standing alone at his post. Jake waves and Lucanus Honorius taps his right fist on the armor

TIME CRASHERS

over his heart and extends his arm. Jake turns away, hurrying to catch up with his friends.

They slog toward the fiery mountain, flames spewing from the peak and scattered blazes flickering on the slopes. Lightning crackles around the crown of Vesuvius, the boom of thunder joining the volcano's roar.

"When we got here yesterday, Pompeii looked like heaven," Ethan says. "Now it looks like the opposite place."

"You mean math class?" Jake asks. Spencer's chuckle breaks into a hacking cough that leaves him gasping for breath.

"These fumes are awful," Ethan sympathizes.

"Poisonous," Spencer wheezes. "Sulfur dioxide, carbon monoxide, hydrogen sulfide, methane—uh-huh, uh-huh—boron, mercury vapor— uh-huh, uh-huh—" The list of poison gases dissolves into more coughing.

"Please stop, Dr. Downer," Jake pleads. "If the gases don't kill us, you'll bore us to death."

After a few more yards struggling uphill, Spencer topples over. Jake catches him before he falls. Pitching the torch to Ethan, Jake lifts Spencer in his arms.

"Hang on, buddy," he whispers. "Not much further."

"Slowing you down," Spencer gasps. "Leave me."

"All for one," Jake says. "Besides, we might need that Tony Stark brain of yours before we get out of here."

They press on, ash raining from above and the ground shaking underfoot.

"We've got trouble," Ethan whispers to Jake. He waves at the smoldering slopes. "The vineyards, the gardens, the olive groves... Everything has burned. I know we're close to where we arrived, but maybe not close enough to pick up the pulse."

"How are we gonna find our place when all the trees are burned to stumps?" Jake moans. "My orange X is buried under a foot of ash."

"Any ideas, Spence?" Ethan asks, but Spencer has fainted.

Jake sags to his knees, propping the unconscious Spencer against his chest. Coney bounds over and licks Spencer's face.

Ethan freezes in his pacing.

"Coney's a hunting dog, right?" Ethan asks.

"Sure," Jake agrees, "but I think he hunts animals, not removal buses."

"He hunts by smell," Ethan exclaims. "Do you still have that can of spray paint?"

"Sure, but—" Jake's face brightens. He digs out the can and sprays his palm. "Take a good whiff, Coney."

The dog sniffs the orange paint and looks up curiously.

"Find that smell," Jake tells him. "Fetch. Hunt. Go!"

Furiously wagging his tail, Coney scents the smoky air. Head down, nose just above the ashes, the Laconian hunter creeps over the ground. He circles, sniffing, pausing, moving on. Now and again he sneezes violently, shakes his head, and returns to the quest.

Minutes drag by. Ethan shuffles off with the torch, following the trail of the meandering dog.

"Come on, Coney, you can do it," Ethan says. The dog glances up, then resumes sniffing over the gray terrain. The volcano rumbles angrily and the dog stiffens. At first Ethan thinks Coney is frightened, but the dog looks up expectantly and holds his pose.

Ethan stoops in front of the hound and frantically brushes ash away.

He uncovers the bold X.

"You did it!" Jake shouts. "God bless that wonderful nose!"

Stabbing the torch into the scorched earth, Ethan runs back along his own tracks in the ash. "Jake! Get it in gear!"

Jake emerges from the darkness, Spencer over his shoulder.

Together they stagger toward the dying torch, arriving as the last flame flickers out.

"Now we wait to see if time is on our side," Ethan says, his voice tired and cracked. "We've done everything we can."

"Almost," Jake says. He lays Spencer on the ground, gently brushing the ashes away from his friend's face. Turning to Coney, Jake takes the dog's head in his hands and looks into the black, sparkling eyes. "Boy, you have to get out of here. If you stay with us, you're going to be the world's original hot dog."

The hound looks at him quizzically, rear end wriggling.

"Run to the city and keep going, Coney," Jake urges. "We'll be okay. You go!" The dog hesitates. "Go! Now!"

Coney licks Jake's hand, yips at Ethan, then wheels toward Pompeii. In seconds he disappears into the darkness.

"That dog is a survivor," Jake says. "It'll take more than a volcano to put Coney down."

They settle onto the trembling ground. The fiery glow from Vesuvius reddens their faces. Bolts of lightning stab their eyes like camera flashes.

"When is the bus coming?" Jake asks.

Ethan shrugs. "This dust ruined my watch."

"Tell me about it," Jake groans. "I think my pockets are filled with twenty pounds of pumice."

Abruptly an explosion rocks the ground. Angry flares leap from Vesuvius. The gusher of flame pushes higher and higher.

"Biggest Roman candle in history," Jake murmurs.

The fiery pillar collapses and a red-orange wave rolls down the mountain.

Spencer sits up, coughing. "Pyroclastic surge," he rasps. "Superheated gases. Five hundred degrees. Vaporizes the flesh on a human body and boils the brain inside the skull."

"We're finished," Ethan says.

"The surge travels roughly one hundred miles an hour. We're about five miles from the peak. So we've got three minutes before …" Spencer's voice trails off.

"If Lucanus Honorius can stand his ground, so can we," Ethan says. "Either the Pulse takes us home or the surge takes us to heaven."

"Yeah!" Jake agrees. "I won't waste my three minutes being scared."

With effort, Spencer climbs to his feet. "When you walk through the fire, you will not be burned; the flames will not set you ablaze," he recites. "For I am the LORD your God …"

Ethan stands next to Spencer and puts an arm around his shoulder. "God is our refuge and strength, an ever-present help in trouble," Ethan says. "Therefore we will not fear, though the earth gives way and the mountains fall into the heart of the sea …"

Jake joins his friends, standing on Spencer's other side. "It's a

great way to die," Jake says. "Way better than slipping on a piece of soap in the shower or choking on a pickle."

A tingle raises hairs on the back of Ethan's neck. The retrieval pulse is energizing, reaching across the centuries.

"Here comes the pulse," Spencer says.

"Too bad, buddy," Ethan says to Jake. "You'll have to find some other cool way to die."

As the tingling grows, the surge rolls closer. The wind rises, whipping the boys' hair. The first heat from the wave slaps their skin.

Sulfur burns their nostrils. The ground rocks and the boys struggle to keep their footing. The shriek of the descending wave drowns every other sound. Ethan expects his cheeks to blister.

"The Pulse is too late," Ethan whispers. "We're going to burn up."

Then the boys disappear, transported safely to the 21st century.

Six seconds later, the pyroclastic surge sweeps away three sets of footprints in the ash.

THE END

SEE EPILOGUE, PAGE 194.

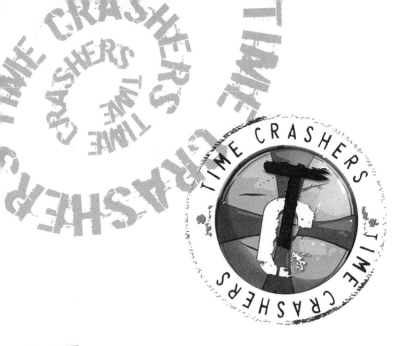

"All right," Ethan gives in. "I picked the grove, you pick the tree."

Still carrying Spencer, Jake starts at the corner of the grove and marches east to the nineteenth tree, then north for five more trees. "Here we are," he says, settling into the ashes with a groan of fatigue. "Now we wait for the pulse."

Ethan flops in the gritty ashes as well. Their eyes turn to the deadly mountain. Fire and smoke belch from the summit. Lightning dances crazily in the sky. Winds rise and fall, whipping ashes into their red eyes.

Minutes tick by.

"Do you think we're in the right place?" Jake wonders.

"I wish we could ask Spencer," Ethan says.

"Omigosh!" Jake explodes. He frantically pats his pockets and pulls out a paper-wrapped cylinder half the length of a crayon. "Smelling salts! This stuff would wake up a mummy."

He holds the tube under Spencer's nose and bends it. Crack! Ammonia seeps into the air. Spencer's eyes fly open and he jerks upright, batting the smelling salts away.

Spencer blinks watery eyes and asks, "Waszh habbening?"

"The verse!" Jake shouts. "Is it Mark 5:19 or 19:5?"

"Go yome to yerown peeples," Spencer mumbles, trying to focus his eyes on Jake.

"That's the one," Jake cries. "Is it Mark 19:5?"

Spencer frowns and waves a hand before his face as if swatting a fly. "Mark only haszh shixteen chappers, dummy." He yawns hugely and falls back to sleep.

"Mark only has sixteen chapters?" Ethan asks. "There's no such verse as Mark 19:5."

"We're at the wrong tree," Jake wails.

Throwing Spencer over his shoulder like a sack of potatoes, Jake runs back through the grove, Ethan close behind. "Five east," he pants. "Nineteen north. This is the one." He drops to his knees beside a charred stump.

Within seconds, they feel an odd tingle ripple over their bodies.

"Hooray," Jake cheers. "Here comes the retrieval pulse."

"You didn't call it the removal bus," Ethan says, puzzled.

"Nah, I just do that to bug Spencer," Jake admits. "Where's the fun if he's asleep?"

A moment later, the boys vanish from the year 79 AD, leaving behind only trampled ashes.

THE END

SEE EPILOGUE, PAGE 194.

I trust your memory more than mine," Jake tells Ethan. "Let's go with Mark 5:19."

They pace five trees to the east, then turn into the remains of the grove and count nineteen burned trees north. They drop exhausted to the ground, and Jake lays Spencer's head in his lap.

"He'll wake up as soon as we get home?" Jake asks.

Ethan nods, almost too tired to talk. "We can't take anything home from the past. That includes the medicine Spencer drank. When we get back, his system will be clean."

"He'll be using long words again, giving us lectures, and correcting everything I say," Jake sighs. "I've missed that."

The two boys high five as the retrieval pulse tickles their skin.

TIME CRASHERS

TIME CRASHERS

A vibration revs in their bellies as the pulse locks on their location. Overhead, Vesuvius stabs a monstrous finger of flame into the black sky, but the Time Crashers are already gone.

THE END

SEE EPILOGUE, PAGE 194.

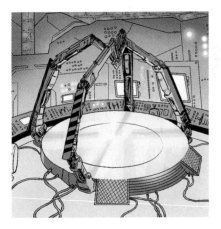

Epilogue

The boys materialize in the dim light of the basement laboratory. Their clothes are rumpled, but all dust and ash have been left in the past. Spencer takes a deep breath. "That fresh air smells sweet."

"Who knew a cool, damp basement could feel so good?" Jake says, stretching and yawning.

"Another failure," Ethan says.

"No way," Spencer argues. "Now we know your dad isn't in ancient Pompeii. Every trip brings us closer to finding him."

Jake says, "I want to know

what happened to you guys while we were scouting solo. You gotta hear my gladiator stories."

"Stick around. We'll debrief," Ethan suggests.

They go upstairs, and Ethan finds Miss Wigger in the kitchen.

"Are you finished so soon?" Miss Wigger asks in surprise. "You've only been working for a few minutes."

"We got a lot done," Ethan assures her. "Can Jake and Spencer stay for dinner?"

"How about a special treat tonight?" Miss Wigger suggests. "I'll get the grill going, and each of you can cook your own burgers."

"You mean with real fire and smoke?" Ethan asks in dismay.

"And red-hot coals?" Jake adds.

"And ashes?" Spencer chimes in.

"Of course," Miss Wigger answers. "How else can you grill hamburgers?"

The boys look at one another uneasily.

"If it's okay with you," Ethan asks, "can we make peanut butter sandwiches?"

"Suit yourself," Miss Wigger says stiffly. "I'll never understand you boys."

"I hope not," Ethan says, winking at his pals.

The Real Deal

Many of the characters in this book were real people in Pompeii. The fuller Vesonius Primus and his wife Cornelia lived in a beautiful home. Commander Pliny really launched a rescue attempt by sea. A Roman guard actually did die on duty at the city gate, although we don't know his name.

All of the graffiti mentioned in this story has been found on the walls of the buried city, as well as a ROTAS square inscribed on a column. (By the way, "May you sneeze sweetly" was how people wished each other good luck.) A funny bit of graffiti is: "Everyone writes on walls— except me." One of the most touching poems written on a public wall was, "Nothing lasts forever; though the sun shines gold, it must sink into the sea." Those lines turned out to be a prediction of the city's sad fate.

Fortunately, most of Pompeii's twenty thousand citizens escaped the eruption in the year 79 AD. Archaeologists have found the remains of about two thousand people buried in the ash of Pompeii. As water trickled through the ashes, the human remains rotted away, leaving hollow molds in the shape of the bodies.

When diggers find those spots, they often pour plaster in, creating casts of long-dead people. These plaster casts show the  poses of dying people in their last moments. Some of these are very sad, like the dog on a chain or the mother and child who died side by side. Some of the dead were found surrounded by gold and silver. Maybe those people could have escaped if they had left their treasures behind.

Even today, nearly two thousand years later, Vesuvius is an active volcano. The most recent eruption in 1944 destroyed three villages. If Vesuvius erupts in our time, over half a million people will have to escape. How do you think that would turn out?

Fiery Fun Answers

■ **DIFFERENT STROKES**

There are different kinds of gifts, but the same Spirit distributes them.

There are different kinds of service, but the same Lord.

(1 Corinthians 12:4-5)

■ **DRESS FOR SUCCESS!**

Belt of truth.

Breastplate of righteousness.

Feet of readiness.

Shield of faith.

Helmet of salvation.

Sword of the Spirit.

■ **TAKE A NUMBER!**

Which Roman numeral can climb a wall?   IV (ivy)

Which Roman numeral belongs on top of a jar?   LID

Which Roman numeral plays music?   CD

Which Roman numeral needs a new light bulb?   DIM

Which Roman numeral did the blind man shout when Jesus healed him?   IC (I see)

What is the favorite Roman numeral of the retired doctor?

Continued on page 200.

XMD

Which Roman numeral did the police officer ask for?   ID

Which Roman numeral is a word in a recipe?   MIX

BRAIN TEASER: 969

■ WILD WHEELS

THE DRIVING IS LIKE THAT OF JEHU SON OF NIMSHI;
HE DRIVES LIKE A MANIAC.

■ PRIDE: TAKE IT OR LEAVE IT?

I DON'T NEED HELP FROM ANYONE. *unhealthy*

I KNOW HOW TO APOLOGIZE WHEN I'M WRONG.
healthy

I BELIEVE GOD LOVES ME JUST THE WAY I AM. *healthy*

I GET ANGRY WHEN I LOSE A GAME. *unhealthy*

I LIKE TO SEE OTHERS DO WELL. *healthy*

I ENJOY DOING THINGS I'M GOOD AT. *healthy*

I THINK SECOND PLACE IS FOR LOSERS. *unhealthy*

I CAN TAKE ADVICE FROM OTHERS. *healthy*

I AM THANKFUL FOR MY BLESSINGS. *healthy*

■ LOVE YOUR NEIGHBOR'S PET?

A RIGHTEOUS MAN CARES FOR THE NEEDS OF HIS
ANIMAL. (Proverbs 12:10)